"Hey," he said softly, drawing her eyes up to meet his.

Jack set a gentle hand over hers and leveled her with his most sincere stare. "You're going to get through this, and you're going to be okay. I won't leave you until I know you're safe and you want me to go. Okay?" And to be honest, he wasn't sure he'd want to go then, either. He traced her porcelain skin with his eyes, noting the feminine lines of her jaw and cheeks, the enticing curve of her neck.

Katlin wet her lips, and Jack allowed himself the indulgence of trailing the path of her tongue with his heated gaze. Allowed himself one moment to imagine the taste of her smooth pink lips under his.

"Jack," she whispered, the sweet sound tightening his muscles impossibly further. "What if I don't remember?"

DANGEROUS KNOWLEDGE

JULIE ANNE LINDSEY

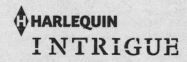

HARLEQUIN
INTRIGUE

To Jack, my home-building hero.

HARLEQUIN®
INTRIGUE®

Recycling programs
for this product may
not exist in your area.

ISBN-13: 978-1-335-13685-5

Dangerous Knowledge

Copyright © 2020 by Julie Anne Lindsey

This edition published by arrangement with Harlequin Books S.A.

For questions and comments about the quality of this book,
please contact us at CustomerService@Harlequin.com.

Harlequin Enterprises ULC
22 Adelaide St. West, 40th Floor
Toronto, Ontario M5H 4E3, Canada
www.Harlequin.com

Printed in U.S.A.

Julie Anne Lindsey is an obsessive reader who was once torn between the love of her two favorite genres: toe-curling romance and chew-your-nails suspense. Now she gets to write both for Harlequin Intrigue. When she's not creating new worlds, Julie can be found carpooling her three kids around northeastern Ohio and plotting with her shamelessly enabling friends. Winner of the Daphne du Maurier Award for Excellence in Mystery/Suspense, Julie is a member of International Thriller Writers, Romance Writers of America and Sisters in Crime. Learn more about Julie and her books at julieannelindsey.com.

Books by Julie Anne Lindsey

Harlequin Intrigue

Fortress Defense

Deadly Cover-Up
Missing in the Mountains
Marine Protector
Dangerous Knowledge

Garrett Valor

Shadow Point Deputy
Marked by the Marshal

Protectors of Cade County

Federal Agent Under Fire
The Sheriff's Secret

Visit the Author Profile page at Harlequin.com.

CAST OF CHARACTERS

Katlin Andrews—Car crash and amnesia victim on the run from an unknown assailant, shooter and relentless hit man who wants something from her she can't recall.

Jack Hale—Fortress Defense member, former Army Ranger and best friend to Katlin's older brother, previously lost in battle. Jack's determined to fulfill Katlin's brother's dying wish by protecting her, whatever comes, while keeping his hands off. And definitely not falling in love.

Wyatt Stone—Former Army Ranger and current cofounder of Fortress Defense, working with his team to defend and protect Katlin while she regains her memories.

Sawyer Lance—Cade's older brother, former Army Ranger and founding member of Fortress Defense.

Cade Lance—Former US Marine and current Fortress Defense team member working to protect Katlin from an unknown assailant and gunman.

Detective Reihl—Local detective assigned to Katlin's case.

Chapter One

Katlin Andrews adjusted her sweaty grip on the steering wheel, smiling wildly as she navigated the dark roads in the worst part of town. She'd single-handedly nailed down the story of a lifetime tonight, and she couldn't wait to see her boss's face when she proved it. He thought she was too young and inexperienced to know a real story if it bit her, but he was wrong. And she hadn't just nailed this one down, she'd blown it wide open.

The thrill of victory rushed through her veins as she made the final turn out of the run-down neighborhood, thankful to be on her way home. Only a few more blocks to the highway, then she'd work until dawn. Put all the puzzle pieces together and tie up every loose ends. The findings from tonight's outing were going to change her life. She was sure of it.

A set of headlights flashed in her rearview mirror, distracting her thoughts and eating up the dark road behind her. Katlin pushed the gas pedal with renewed purpose, her intuition spiking. No one out at this hour, in this area, could be up to anything good, and she certainly didn't want to think about the reason a car was racing after her tonight.

Didn't want to think that maybe she'd been caught.

Katlin wet her lips and divided her attention between the dark road before her and the glaring headlights behind her. Maybe she was wrong. Maybe the car would just pass by. Maybe she was overreacting. She certainly hadn't seen anyone watching as she'd crept through the decrepit basement window and snooped around the overfilled space, taking photos to prove her suspicions.

Still, the headlights drew nearer rapidly, until they became one blinding spotlight that caused Katlin to squint and swerve. She urged the pedal lower, a sheen of sweat forming on her upper lip. With a mighty roar of the engine, the assailing car nudged her little sedan's rear bumper and she skidded sideways along the desolate road.

Katlin screamed and her heart raced as she struggled to regain control of the vehicle. She didn't know how, but she'd definitely been caught. The maniac behind her surged forward again, bumping her harder this time and causing her to clip an orange-and-white construction barrel beside the freeway's entrance.

She steered her vehicle back between the lines, then fumbled for her cell phone. The birthday card she'd been carrying with her for nearly two years fell from her purse in the process, but she didn't need the card anymore. She'd long ago memorized the number inside. Her brother had trusted Jack Hale with his life, and that was all Katlin needed to know.

She worked to dial the number while staying on the road and keeping watch over the car advancing and retreating behind her. Taunting her in maddening waves.

The call connected then rang, with long, infuriating pauses between. Katlin's eyes blurred with tears of desperation. "Come on," she whispered. "Pick up. Pick up. Pick up."

"You've reached Jack Hale," a low, authoritative tenor announced. "Leave a message."

"Dammit." Katlin ended the call and immediately tried again.

The pursuing car slid into the empty passing lane then sailed effortlessly into position beside her. Its sleek silver paint made it look like a bullet in the night.

"You've reached Jack Hale..."

Katlin ended the call and redialed. One more time, then she'd leave a detailed message. That would be better than nothing. In the event she didn't survive the night, at least someone she could trust would be able to relay what she knew, and the son of a gun trying to kill her would be punished.

The silver car swerved sharply in her direction, and Katlin pulled hard on the steering wheel. Her fender nicked the guardrail with a hellacious screech and a jolt that nearly knocked the phone from her hand as she pressed Call one last time.

"Come on," she whispered. To the phone. To the universe. "Come on."

She smashed her toe against the gas pedal, steering wildly and one-handed as she raced along the narrow berm, dirt and pebbles flying into the air behind her. "Please," she begged. "Pick up, Jack. I need you. Pick. Up!" A lump formed in Katlin's throat as she listened to the slow, tinny rings.

"You've reached…"

A bone-jarring thump knocked the phone from her hand. The assailing car pressed against her door, forcing her farther off the road. She stomped the brake pedal and pulled the steering wheel hard, shoving back against the attacking vehicle and away from the thin metal guardrail. The silver car relented for one fleeting heartbeat, then returned with a teeth-rattling *whack*!

And Katlin careened over the road's edge.

Airborne and plummeting toward the river below.

THE PHONE BEGAN to ring again as Jack stepped out of the shower. Being the last man on-site at Fortress Defense, the private protection firm he'd started with his brothers-in-arms, made catching a nap, having a meal and apparently taking a shower nearly impossible. Office hours had ended well before his evening return, and he'd just wrapped his last case only hours before, but duty, it seemed, never stopped calling. Jack had anticipated some quiet time while he filed paperwork, hit the agency's gym and caught a shower, but that hadn't happened. Especially odd since the emergency line was set to go to Sawyer's phone tonight. Instead the ringing had persisted off and on, from the minute he'd finished his postcase workout and started the shower until he'd stepped out and wrapped a towel around his hips. Now, bare-foot in jeans and hunting for a shirt, the ringing had begun again.

He grabbed his cell phone and read the screen. Seven missed calls. Three from the same unknown number, a little over an hour ago. He'd missed those completely. Probably while he'd been working out. And four more calls from the blocked number call-ing in now.

"Fortress Defense," he answered, gripping the phone to his ear in one hand and knocking water from his hair with the other. "You've got Jack Hale."

"Mr. Hale, this is Detective Reihl from the Camp-bellsville Police Department," an unfamiliar woman's voice explained.

Jack stilled, a tendril of dread curling in his stom-ach. Civilians called when they needed protection. Law-enforcement officers called when it was already too late. "What's this about?" He strained to recall a client who lived or worked in Campbellsville. Where was Campbellsville? East? South?

"This is about a car accident on Highway 68 to-night," the detective answered. "Near an exit down-town. Are you familiar with the area?"

"No, ma'am," he said, finding and tugging a T-shirt over still-damp skin. "Was a Fortress Defense client involved in the crash? Is everyone okay?" He selected a pen from the mug on his desk and poised it over a pad of paper, ready to take down the de-tails for whichever one of his teammates was about to get bad news. It wasn't him. He'd never had a client from Campbellsville.

"Well, I'm afraid you're going to have to tell me," Reihl said. "The driver called your number repeatedly in the final minutes before her car left the road."

"My number?" Jack asked, setting aside the pen. His gaze landed on the silent cell phone on the charger across the room. The company phone. The phone pressed against his ear was his personal device. "And you said the crash was tonight?" he asked, recalling the other set of missed calls. Three from the same unknown number. "About an hour ago?"

"That's right," Detective Reihl said, a note of curiosity in her tone. "Any idea what that was about? Why she would've called you so many times while racing along the highway? Angry girlfriend, or an ex, perhaps? Maybe the two of you had a fight and she was all worked up?"

Jack shook his head, stretching socks over his feet and stuffing them into unlaced boots. "No girlfriend." The only woman he'd ever loved had died in a training exercise over Somalia four years ago. He wasn't interested in knowing loss like that again. "Who was she?" he asked. "The woman in the accident." Whoever she was, she'd wanted to talk to him, and he wanted to know why. "She's okay?" he asked, realizing the detective hadn't answered him before.

"Okay is subjective," Reihl said. "Kentucky driver's license says she's Katlin Andrews. Know her now?"

Jack felt the air press from his lungs. "Katlin Andrews?" he asked, his ears ringing. He was certain he'd heard wrong.

"Uh-huh. Twenty-six, blond hair, brown eyes. Stop me if I'm ringing a bell because she clearly knew you and really wanted to have a chat."

Jack forced back the ache of emotion and rising bile. Katlin was hurt. She'd called him for help, and he hadn't answered. "Where is she now? Can I see her?"

"I suppose," the detective answered. "Doctors seem to think she's fine, or that she will be. Hard to say for sure. She's been out cold since she got here. I can't talk to her, so I thought I'd talk to you. You do know her then?"

Relief flooded his limbs and lightened his head. "Not really. She's my best friend's baby sister, and I suppose I'm her unofficial guardian."

"So the brother is her next of kin? Can you tell me how to get in touch with him?"

"No, ma'am," Jack replied, then cleared his throat. His muscles stiffened in preparation for the coming words. "Griffin Andrews is dead." Lost during a reconnaissance mission three years back. "He and I were stationed abroad together for four years. We were family. For all intents and purposes. When I lost him, I gained her. You understand?"

"Like a replacement brother?"

"Yes, ma'am." Though he'd been a lousy one so far. Not such a great one before, either. The first time he'd seen a photo of Katlin he'd whistled and complimented Griffin on his smoking-hot girlfriend, then barely dodged a blow aimed at his nose. The way Griffin had spoken about her before that, Jack had expected Katlin to be in middle school, or even kindergarten, not in daisy dukes and cowgirl boots on Griffin's arm at a country-music concert.

Griffin had laughed when he'd missed his mark. "That's my sister," he'd warned, a very serious threat in his eyes. "You touch her over my dead body."

Jack's heart tightened at the memory. *Over his dead body.* What Jack wouldn't give to have Griffin back. Nothing. There was nothing he wouldn't do.

"I'm sorry for both your losses," Detective Reihl said finally. "Losing a sibling isn't easy. Neither is losing a friend."

Jack pocketed his keys then grabbed his sidearm and holster.

"Do you know how we can get in touch with Miss Andrews's next of kin? A parent or other blood sibling, perhaps?"

"Her folks are stationed in Austria. They're hard to reach. Sometimes impossible. Griffin was her only sibling."

Katlin was on her own in the States. Had been for a long while. And Jack had vowed to look after her for Griffin as he'd taken his last breath. Jack had promised, but he'd never gotten up the nerve to call or stop by her place. He didn't want to be a catalyst to all the emotions that came with the loss of a sibling, especially one as close as Griffin was to Katlin. Instead Jack had just kept sending useless holiday and birthday cards. He'd written his number in every one. Letting her take the lead and decide if she wanted to meet him or not. "It's just me," he said. Unfortunately for Katlin. "Will I be able to see her? Talk to her?"

"You'll have to work that out with the hospital," Detective Reihl said. "I'd like to talk to you in person, if you've got time. Feel up for a trip to Campbellsville tomorrow?"

Jack tugged a plain black ball cap over still-damp hair and threaded eager arms into his trademark leather jacket. "Yep."

He was already on his way.

Chapter Two

Jack made it to Campbellsville in significantly less time than the GPS had predicted. He'd ignored speed limits and taken liberties on the quiet country roads outside town. If there was an upside to the late-night call, it was traveling while everyone else was in bed. Traffic was something he didn't have time for tonight.

The hospital loomed tall and bright above the sparse cityscape, impossible to miss as he navigated through the sleepy town. He chose a front-row parking spot, then headed for the emergency-room doors. The woman behind the check-in desk looked up as he approached.

"I'm here for Katlin Andrews," he said. Images of the beautiful, healthy blonde swept into mind once more. Pictures of her and Griffin with family and friends. At the beach, on a boat, at concerts and graduations. The familiar prints had hung from his best friend's locker for years. Photos Jack had packed up to send home following his tragic loss. "She was in a car accident. Detective Reihl called me about two hours ago."

The nurse appraised him. "You family?"

"Yes," he said, having rehearsed the story on his way in. He and Katlin weren't blood-related, but Jack had made a vow to watch over her, and he couldn't do that if he wasn't allowed to see her.

"Third floor," she said, satisfied with his lie. "Trauma ward, but—"

"Thank you." Jack didn't have time to stick around for cautions or warnings. He needed to be present when Katlin woke. No one should be alone after what she'd been through. He jogged toward the stairs with renewed purpose.

"Visiting hours are over," the nurse called as the stairwell door swung shut behind him.

He took the steps two at a time, the sounds of his footfalls echoing off the stark white walls. Memories of another hospital pushed to the surface of his mind. Losing the only woman he'd ever loved had nearly cost him his sanity. Griffin had sat with him then, one protective arm around his shoulders while Jack fought the blinding tears of a gut-wrenching heartache. He gritted his teeth and willed away the memory. This wasn't a military base and Katlin wasn't another soldier. Jack's heart was no longer broken and would never be left unguarded again.

He exited the empty stairwell into a just-as-quiet hallway, the air tinged with bleach and latex. Pale green walls and a speckled tile floor led him to the nurses' desk, where a pair of women in scrubs were speaking in hushed tones over steaming coffees and an open laptop.

The women started when they noticed him.

"Sorry," he said softly, raising his palms in a movement he hoped would put them at ease. "I didn't mean to startle you. I know it's late, but Katlin Andrews was in a car accident tonight. I came as soon as Detective Reihl contacted me."

The nurses' postures and expressions relaxed by a fraction. The little blonde, whose name tag said Julia, worked up a polite smile. "Of course." She stood and moved a clipboard in his direction. "We keep a record of all the visitors on this floor." She gave him a searching look, then a pen. "Visiting hours don't begin again until eight a.m., and we limit those to family only. It's my understanding that Miss Andrews's family lives abroad."

"They do," Jack answered on instinct, then kicked himself for forgetting his lines. "I'm Jack Hale. Katlin's...fiancé." The final word tasted like betrayal, a nonsensical affront to his love for Cara, but painful nonetheless.

Julia clutched her hands to her chest and her bottom lip jutted out. "I'm sorry. No one told us she was engaged."

"It's fine," he said, glad to put the lie behind him. "It's been a hard night. A lot's happened."

The second nurse's brow furrowed. "Katlin Andrews wasn't wearing an engagement ring."

"It's new," Jack improvised, officially disliking Nurse Two. "We've talked about marriage for a while, but we haven't made it official. *I*..." he amended. "*I* haven't made it official, and I should have. I need to get her a ring."

"Darn right you better," Nurse Two said. "She could've died without ever knowing you were serious about that ringless proposal."

"Absolutely," Jack agreed. "I'll make it right as soon as I can." Those words came easier. They were true. He would make things right for Katlin when she woke. He'd do whatever was necessary so that she would recover fully and fast. He owed Griffin that.

Julia smiled. "Miss Andrews is still unconscious, but we do rounds regularly. We'll let you know if anything changes." She pointed at the clipboard. "If you could just sign in before taking a seat, you're welcome to wait."

"Thanks." Jack lifted the pen, then checked his watch. "Any chance Detective Reihl is around?"

"Doubtful," Julia said, "but I expect she'll be back."

Good. Jack had about a thousand questions for the detective, beginning with the basics. How fast was Katlin going when she crashed? Were there any witnesses? Could she have fallen asleep at the wheel? All things he hadn't thought to ask until he'd been well on his way to Campbellsville. He raised his eyes to the waiting nurses before him. "Have you ordered a tox screen?"

Julia nodded. "We should have the results back later today."

"Can you tell me anything about the accident?" he asked.

"Sorry, but no. I suspect Katlin is the only one who can do that, and she's been unresponsive since her arrival."

Nurse Two folded her hands on the desk and leaned toward him conspiratorially. "I heard the detective talking to an officer when Miss Andrews was first admitted. The officer said her car was at the police impound lot, and there was some damage to the driver's side and rear bumper. Strange for a car that went headfirst toward the river. That's on the right side of the highway."

Jack widened his stance and crossed his arms, clipboard pinched between a thumb and forefinger. "You think someone hit her? Forced her off the road?"

Julia shrugged. "We've speculated. She was outside a pretty rough part of town. Could be she was nicked by someone who wasn't in any condition to drive."

Jack certainly preferred that to the possibility Katlin had been driving under the influence, but why would Katlin have been in a seedy part of Campbellsville? Why was she in Campbellsville at all? He'd been sending her cards to Stanford, at least an hour away. "Detective Reihl said she was near an exit when she crashed. Do you know which one?"

"One-nineteen," Julia said. "It's the only place where the river runs along the highway."

"And the impound lot?" Jack asked. "Do you have an address? I'd like to pay both a visit."

Julia wrinkled her nose. "Impound lot's on Main near the police station. It opens early, but you've got another couple of hours before sunup."

"Right." Jack looked around the empty waiting area behind him, rubbing his palms along the sides of his pants. "Care if I stay here until visiting hours begin, or until Katlin wakes?" he asked. "You'll let me know if she does? Even if it's before eight?"

"Sure." Julia smiled sweetly. "You can take a seat. We won't tell if you don't. I'm going to make my rounds now. If she wakes, I'll let you know."

Jack lowered himself into a chair beside a large window, angling for a view of the desk, elevator and stairs. And fought the urge to follow Julia down the hall to Katlin.

KATLIN SQUIRMED AGAINST an uncomfortable ache in her side and a slow pounding in her head. The world was too bright, her eyes scratchy and dry. Her limbs were heavy. Her thoughts awash. She squinted at the fluorescent lights overhead. Where was she?

"Oh!" A perky voice sounded nearby, drawing her attention to a petite blonde wearing blue scrubs and a smile. "Hello, Katlin." She moved closer and reached for Katlin's wrist. "You've been sleeping a long while. We were beginning to wonder when you planned to wake up."

Katlin resisted the urge to pull her arm away. She

scanned the room instead. A hospital. And a nurse. The badge on the woman's chest said Julia.

Why was she in a hospital? She raked her memory, but came up with nothing. She didn't recall being hurt, yet her limbs ached and her throat was painfully dry. "I've been sleeping a while?" she croaked, not recognizing the voice that resulted.

"Several hours," Julia said. She released Katlin's wrist, then reached for a notepad in her pocket and made a note. "You were in an accident last night. Do you remember?"

"No." She cleared her throat several times, unable to remove the strange thickness inside. "What kind of accident?"

Julia's sharp blue eyes snapped to meet hers. "A car accident. Honey, you ran off the road on Highway 68. Nearly landed in the river. We're still not quite sure how you walked away with so many minor injuries."

Katlin's heart rate spiked and a vague sense of foreboding wiggled over her skin, raising gooseflesh in its wake. "What happened?"

"We were hoping you'd tell us." Julia played with the machines arranged near the head of Katlin's bed, a mischievous smile spreading her thin lips. "What I do know is that your dead-sexy boyfriend is in the waiting room, and he's determined to find out how you got hurt. He's a little intense, and I've got to be honest. I feel bad for anyone he thinks might've been involved. But he's sweet, too. Worried sick about you and ready to go charging into the night in search of justice for his honey. He'll be thrilled to hear you're up."

"Boyfriend?" Katlin tried and failed to recall having one of those. Then, she tried and failed to recall anything at all, and a fresh surge of panic welled in her.

"It's just not fair," Julia mused. "Where on earth did you find him? I want one. Hell, every woman I know wants one."

Katlin shook her head. None of this was right. She didn't have a boyfriend. She didn't have an accident. She needed to leave. To move. To hide.

But from what? From whom?

She raised a hand to her temple and froze when an IV line came into view. "What is this? I don't want this."

Julia pressed Katlin's hand gently down. "It's fluids and medicine for the pain. You need both."

"I want to go home." Another flare of panic lit in her core. *Where was home?* Surely she had a home. Didn't she?

The nurse watched her carefully, narrow eyebrows pulling tight. "Honey, it's okay to relax. You're going to be just fine. Your vitals are strong. You only needed a few stitches and a little observation. You'll probably be released this morning."

Katlin's chest constricted further and her tongue seemed to swell. *Released to go where?*

A soft knock sounded against the doorjamb, and a man in his late twenties peered inside. He wore a black ball cap and leather jacket, nice-fitting jeans, boots and a pained expression on his brutally hand-some face. The scruff on his cheeks suggested he hadn't shaved in at least a week, and the fear in his eyes said he was worried. About her? Was this her boyfriend?

If not, she had an idea of where Julia could find herself a smoking-hot man.

Whoever he was, Julia could have him. Katlin needed to get out of there. The pooling sense of dread had filled her stomach and was quickly spreading through her limbs and into her pounding heart. She might not remember how to get home, but she was certain she shouldn't stay here.

"Hey," he said softly, hazel eyes fixed on Julia. "How's she doing?"

Julia glanced at the nearby machines, where Katlin's climbing heart rate was being broadcast. "She seems a little confused, but certainly glad to see you." She hooked a thumb in the machine's direction and cast him a knowing smile.

His gaze flickered briefly in the direction she indicated, then fixed on Katlin's face. A strange mix of emotions raced across the rugged features. Fear? Dismay? Urgency. She was sure about the last one, not as much about the others. And maybe it was all just the projection of her jangled nerves.

"How soon can I leave?" she asked, refocusing on Julia.

"I'll page Dr. Kraus and be right back," she said, stepping into the doorway where the man lingered. "You can go on in."

He waited for her to pass before crossing the threshold with an apologetic smile. "Hi," he said, removing his hat and clutching it to his chest. "I'm Jack Hale."

Katlin stared. "That's a strange way for a boyfriend to introduce himself."

He smiled. "Right. Sorry about that. How are you feeling?"

Awful. Achy. Terrified. "Okay."

"Do you remember me?" he asked. "Recognize my name?"

She shook her head, unwilling to admit the truth. Not only did she not remember this man's name, but she also couldn't recall her own. "What happened to me?"

Jack moved closer, taking slow, calculated steps. "That's what I plan to find out." He stopped at the bedside, staring down at her as if she held the answer to something she couldn't fathom.

"So you're my boyfriend?"

A mischievous half smile tilted his lips. "Hospital policy says only family can visit you, and since your family isn't here, I figured it was okay for me to tell a little white lie. No sense in you being all alone when I was right outside."

"So you're not my boyfriend," she said, flatly, only interested in facts. "Then who are you?" Katlin ran a quick internal inventory, searching for signs she should fear him, but found none. Instead, there was an odd familiarity.

His eyes narrowed, crinkling the tanned skin at

the corners. "Did you think I might be your boy-friend?"

Katlin sank her teeth into her bottom lip, eyes stinging with nonsensical emotion. "The nurse said…"

"And you assumed? You don't remember?"

Katlin shook her head.

Jack ran a hand over his shorn sandy hair, then gripped the back of his neck. "You would've gone home with anyone who showed up and said they were your boyfriend?" He crossed his arms and frowned, working out the thing she hadn't yet been brave enough to say. "What do you remember exactly?"

Her clogged throat seemed to tighten. "Nothing," she whispered.

Jack eased onto the mattress by her knees and turned intense, soulful eyes on her. "Did you tell the nurse?"

"No."

He pressed his lips into a thin line and gave one stiff dip of his chin. "All right." His tone grew composed and compassionate. "You need to tell her when she comes back. Tell the doctor when he gets here."

"Who are you?" she asked, pushing her chin higher. "You're not my boyfriend, and you said I don't have family here. So why should I listen to you?" Not that she didn't agree with him or think it was logical to confess all of any patient's symptoms to the medical team in charge of his or her care. It just didn't feel like the right thing to do in her case. In fact, the only thing that seemed like the right thing to do now was leave. The notion was intense and instinctual. She didn't want to ignore it. *Couldn't* ignore it. "Answer me so we can leave."

He cocked his head, considering her a moment. "My name is Jack Hale. I was your brother's best friend until his death three years ago. You remember Griffin?"

"No."

Jack's lips turned down, disappointment briefly coloring his cheeks. Then he regrouped. "I promised him I'd look after you, and I'm trying now, but this is the first time we've met."

She blinked. "We've never met?"

"No, but I know you, through your brother. The same way you know me. And I send you cards on your birthday and Christmas. I write my number below my signature and figure you'd reach out to me if you ever needed anything or wanted to meet. According to a local detective, you were calling me around the time of your accident. I can only assume that means you were in trouble."

Katlin tried to process the heap of information while battling her growing urge to flee. "Why would I call you and not the police if I was in trouble, and you and I have never met?"

"The detective says you were speeding. Maybe whatever you were running from had to do with the police. I'm not sure, but I will find out. I started a private protection firm called Fortress Defense with some of my military brothers, and I think that might be why you called."

"I needed protection."

"Maybe." He nodded. "You and Griffin were close. He trusted me, so you would, too."

She didn't remember having a brother, but something about Jack put her mind and muscles at ease. His face and voice didn't hurt the cause. "That's why the nurse said you were going to investigate. It's what you do at your protection firm?"

"We do whatever it takes to protect our clients," he said simply. "Knowing all the facts helps. You can't provide them, so I'll have to get them myself. I'll come back for you when I finish. I can drive you home after you're discharged." Jack stretched onto his feet and made a move for the door.

"No!" Katlin's hand snapped out, curling desperate fingers around his wrist. "Don't leave me. You have to take me with you. Get me out of here." She loosened her grip when he turned back in her direction.

"Why?"

"I can't explain it, and I don't remember the details of what happened, but I think you're right. Someone tried to hurt me. And maybe it's the pain meds or the trauma talking, but I feel strongly that I should get out of here before whoever it was finds me again. I don't want to stick around hoping I'm wrong."

Jack grimaced. "How do you know I'm not the one you should be afraid of?"

Katlin laughed, a hearty, unplanned sound. "If you are, then I'm in more trouble than I thought.

My instincts are the only things I've got to keep me alive right now."

His expression softened a bit. "Not true," he said, pulling a wallet from his back pocket. "You've got me, and you can trust me. I can keep you safe." He flipped open the wallet and removed a well-worn photo, then passed it to her. "This is you and your brother when you were small. Griffin carried it with him everywhere, but it was left behind when they shipped his body home." Jack's Adam's apple bobbed, the movement long and slow. He cleared his throat before powering on. "I've carried that picture with me for three years so I could give it to you one day. Griffin saved my life more than once and in more than one way. I owe it to him to protect you, and I will. Whatever it takes, I'm your man."

Katlin sat straighter, his words an inexplicable balm to her nerves. She might not have her memories, but everything he'd said rang true in her heart, if not familiar in her mind. As a bonus, everything about Jack Hale indicated he was fully capable of keeping his promise, and every part of her was interested in seeing that come true. "Help me find my clothes?"

Chapter Three

Jack turned away in search of Katlin's things, thankful she'd chosen to trust him. What could he have done otherwise? Attempted to protect her from afar? All while trying not to be arrested for stalking? The thought itched in his mind. Why had she called him instead of the police last night?

He cast a furtive look in her direction. What kind of trouble was she in that she wouldn't want the police involved? And what could make anyone want to hurt her? She seemed so small and breakable, especially now with her chin and arms peppered with scrapes and bruises. The fact she'd nearly been killed only hours before tightened a knot in his core and set his jaw on lock. That she was holding herself together, looking determined and confident despite the pain she must be in, without her family or memories to support and guide her, suggested the petite woman he'd sworn to protect was far tougher than she appeared.

He circled the room in search of her personal things, glad to put some distance between himself and Griffin's little sister. Seeing nothing that looked as if it might belong to her, he ducked into the attached restroom for a peek there.

The bathroom was empty. No shoes or clothing. No purse or phone.

Jack took a beat to center himself before returning to Katlin. There was something about her that confused and unsettled him. Not the kind of sensations he wanted to deal with right now. He blamed the lack of sleep and back-to-back cases, something he normally avoided. He needed downtime to stay sharp, but he'd have to do without for now. It was already 6:00 a.m. If they wanted to slip away from the hospital before the sun was up, they'd need to get out within the hour. The sooner, the better.

"Knock, knock," Julia chirped, drawing Jack back through the bathroom doorway as she sashayed into Katlin's room. "Look who I found just starting her morning shift." She swung an arm wide, like a game-show hostess, to indicate the woman in a white lab coat at her side. "It's Dr. Kraus, and she has excellent news."

"Miss Andrews," the doctor said, barely glancing away from the computer in her hands. "You took quite a spill last night. We're glad to see you up. How are you feeling? Mind if I take a look?" She set the device on the nightstand before Katlin answered either question, then began a physical examination.

Jack moved to Julia's side. "Katlin's asking for her things. Do you know where they are?"

Julia smiled. "Sure. I have them in a bag at the

nurses' station, but the clothes are a mess. Blood," she said, whispering the last word. "She can wear a set of my scrubs home, if she'd like. It looks like she's about my size." Julia headed for the hallway.

Jack followed, unsure how much he had a right to know about Katlin's care and condition now that she was awake and able to speak for herself. He hoped she'd take his advice and tell Dr. Kraus about her memory loss. He didn't want to snitch and make an enemy of her already, but he wasn't above doing whatever it took to be sure she was okay.

"Here you go," Julia said, returning a moment later with a pair of large zipper-sealed bags. "That's everything they took off of her at Admissions."

"Thanks."

"And here are those scrubs I promised." She stacked a set of powder-pink nurse attire atop the bags with sneakers, a purse, jacket and other clothing.

He dipped his chin in thanks, then passed the doctor on his way back into the room.

Katlin was seated on the bed, a grimace of discomfort on her face. "She said I can go."

Jack set the pile of items on the bed near Katlin's hand. "What did she say about your head and the memory loss?"

"She says I'm fine. Discharge paperwork is being processed. I'm supposed to take it easy for a few days and let her know if my pain becomes unbearable, or if any new symptoms develop." She pushed aside the scrubs and dug into the plastic bags, then frowned at the bloodstains on her clothes. She gave the pink scrubs a second look, then fanned out her stained jeans in front of her and slipped her feet into the leg holes.

Jack spun around, allowing her some privacy. "Okay, but what did she say about the amnesia?"

"She says it isn't uncommon following a trauma."

Jack peeked over his shoulder. "She doesn't want to keep you for observation?"

"No, and I think that's for the best." She stuffed her bare feet into sneakers, having already pulled the jeans over her hips and fastened them. Her expression fell as she gave the bloodstained shirt a second look. She stuffed it back into the bag with a sigh and lifted the pink scrubs top with a frown. "I think we should get out of here. I've had a lingering feeling of dread since I woke, and I don't think it's a coincidence or strictly a result of the accident. I want to go somewhere I can think and try to remember what's going on."

Jack turned back to face her. "We should start with your apartment. Maybe something there will kick-start your memory."

She nodded, then raised a tentative hand in his direction, her cheeks suddenly tinged with pink. "Okay. I just need to finish getting ready."

Jack followed her gaze to the pink top and a lacy red bra, barely concealed beneath it in her other hand. An image of Katlin in the bra alone rushed into his mind, unbidden, and he rocked back on his heels, reminding himself of the long list of reasons he needed to tighten up.

"I'm back!" Julia reappeared with a digital tablet and a wheelchair. "Just a few signatures here, and you're free to go." She handed Jack the tablet, then detached Katlin's IV and other monitors. "Would you like a set of pain pills before you go?" she asked, smoothing a Band-Aid over Katlin's hand where the IV had been. "It's better to stay ahead of the pain. There's a prescription for more with your discharge papers."

Katlin blushed, the shirt and bra still clutched in her free hand.

Jack sighed. "Give us just a minute." He reached for Katlin and pulled her onto her feet, then guided her across the floor to the bathroom. "You okay?"

She closed her eyes, then shut the door between them in answer.

He did his best not to ask if she needed any help in there.

KATLIN FINISHED DRESSING, then splashed water on her face and finger-combed her hair while searching her empty head for a memory. *Any* memory. Something to make her feel real and anchored instead of adrift like a two-dimensional drawing snipped free of its paper. A fresh wave of emotion slapped into her, and she gave in to it behind the closed door. When the tears had gone dry, she washed her face, squared her shoulders and lifted her chin, then returned to the unfamiliar world outside.

Jack stood at attention beside the wheelchair, clearly awaiting her return. He scanned her carefully, then reached for her hand. "Let me help."

Katlin steered out of his reach as she climbed into the waiting wheelchair. "I've got it, thanks." She was sore and shaken, but she was tougher than all that, and Jack didn't need to know what a mess she truly was. He was her lifeline. Between the two of them they would figure everything out. As long as she made it out of the hospital.

Jack took the hint and gave her some space. He passed the black motorcycle jacket to her that had been with the pile of her things. "Everything okay?" he asked. "You were in there a while."

Katlin fixed him with a warning look as she threaded her arms into the cool leather. "I'm fine. Just moving a little slowly. Where's the nurse?"

He moved into position behind her, taking the handles of the chair in his hands. "Called away. We're completing the discharge process at the desk now." He turned them in the direction of the door and wheeled her into the hallway. "Maybe you should spend the day recuperating instead of investigating. We can always start tomorrow."

"No." She groaned, trying to get comfortable in the chair. "I don't think we have that kind of time. I need my memories back before whoever came at me last night comes again."

"No one's coming for you on my watch," Jack said.

Katlin appreciated the confidence, but she wasn't

so sure. She tried again to access the lost memories. They seemed to hover just outside her reach. Like vapor, she could see and sense them, but not get a hold.

A gray-haired nurse smiled at them over the big wooden desk as they approached. "Ready to go home?"

"Yes," Katlin answered enthusiastically, realizing too late that the question had probably been rhetorical.

"Then let's get started." The nurse turned a digital tablet in Katlin's direction, then guided her through the discharge process before handing her a sheet of printed care instructions and a prescription for more pain pills.

A young woman in scrubs and a volunteer tag came to relieve Jack of his duties. "Hospital policy," she said cheerfully, her gaze raking appreciatively over his lean, muscular form. When her eyes met Katlin's, she blushed.

Jack walked at Katlin's side down the corridor to the elevator, his attention constantly swiveling to take in everything around them. His arm swung wide to stop the wheelchair as a door opened on her opposite side.

Dr. Kraus stepped through the doorway and frowned, dragging her gaze briefly from the laptop in her hands. Her expression deepened at the sight of them. "I didn't know you were still here," she said, fixing her gaze on Katlin. "I just sent your brother out to the parking deck looking for the two of you."

Katlin's breath caught as she swung her attention to Jack. He'd said her brother was dead.

The stiff set of Jack's jaw and cold glare in his eyes sent a shiver down her spine. "Her brother is dead," he said sharply. "What did this man look like? Which way did he go?"

The doctor's mouth opened and shut. Her attention lifted and stuck to Jack for a long moment. "I don't know," she finally answered, clearly baffled.

Jack set his massive hands against his sides and glowered. "Well, that's fantastic and extremely helpful. Thank you." He dismissed the doctor, then took the helm at Katlin's wheelchair, effectively discharging the young volunteer, as well. "I've got it from here. Thanks."

He rushed Katlin to the elevator and jammed his finger against the small button to call the car. When the doors opened, Jack maneuvered her quickly inside. "I don't know who came here looking for you, but it wasn't your brother," he said sternly. "I saw the doubt in your eyes out there, and I want you to know—you have no other family in this country that I'm aware of, none Griffin ever mentioned, anyway. Regardless, anyone who knew you would have known Griffin is gone. I think it's fair to say your instincts were right. We need to get out of here."

Fear chewed at Katlin's gut, constricting her breaths and heating her chest.

"We'll have to walk to my truck," Jack continued. "I hate parking decks. I took a spot on the street around the far side of the building, where visibility is good and we can pull away quick. I can carry you if you aren't feeling up for the walk."

Katlin raised her chin and didn't speak. She'd already told him she was fine, and given the unknown man who was now looking for her, she didn't want to risk her voice cracking or quaking while she tried to set Jack straight.

"Don't say you're fine again," he said, interrupting her thoughts. "You could've been killed last night, and whatever you did to your head knocked your memories out. None of that is good, and I'm not joking about carrying you."

"I can walk," she snapped, unsure it was true. Getting dressed was tough enough. How far away was his truck? "And memories don't work like that," she went on, venting the tension through her words. "I'm not a faulty flashlight. You can't just whack my head again and the light will return. It's a trauma thing. I know the memories are there, I just have to figure out what I can do to trigger them."

Jack gave a puff of air behind her, a soft derisive sound. "Are you trying to convince me? Or yourself?"

"Shut up."

The quirk of his lips reflected in the shiny elevator doors.

She forced away her eyes. Was this normal for her? Did she typically become enamored with any handsome man who was nice to her? She didn't think so, but how could she know? The thought brought another disturbing possibility to mind. "What if I have a real boyfriend?"

The doors parted and Jack hesitated before pushing Katlin out of the elevator. "What do you mean?"

"Well, won't he be mad that you showed up to play hero? Steal his thunder. All that."

Jack parked the wheelchair near the sliding hospital doors, where at least a dozen other wheelchairs were lined against a wall. He moved around to face her and offered her a hand up. "If I was you, and there was some guy out there claiming to be my boyfriend who hadn't bothered to come to the hospital or look for me when I didn't call to say I'd made it home safely last night, I wouldn't care if he was mad. I wouldn't even know he was mad because he'd be out on the curb."

"Harsh." She pressed onto her feet without accepting his hand. "Kick him to the curb? That's your philosophy? No opportunity for explanations?"

Jack shrugged, then matched her tortoise-slow pace along the sidewalk, away from the hospital. "I'm not an easy guy."

"Fair enough," she said, passing men and women in suits and scrubs headed to and from off-site parking. Apparently it was time for a shift change. "Do you hold your girlfriend to the same rules?"

"No." He slid cool hazel eyes in her direction quickly, then returned them to the circuit he seemed to be making—scanning the street, buildings and folks around them. "No girlfriend."

Katlin opened her mouth to ask how that was possible, but the words were interrupted.

"Katlin Andrews," an unfamiliar voice called, making her turn around.

A dark figure peered down from the top floor of the open four-level parking deck. In one swift movement, the figure raised an arm, and the unmistakable sound of gunfire rang out.

Chapter Four

"Get down!" Jack called, grabbing Katlin and tucking her against him as he began to run. "Shots fired!" he screamed at the smattering of confused onlookers, who were taking phone calls and cigarette breaks around the property's edge.

Another shot rang out, and the sidewalk cracked in front of them, sending a tiny puff of dust into the air.

Behind them, people screamed.

Katlin struggled against Jack's protective grip. "I'm okay!" she yelled, pressing him back with her elbows. "Let's go!"

Jack released her, and she bolted for his truck.

He fumbled for the key fob, remotely unlocking the door a heartbeat before they dove in.

"Get down!" he yelled as he cranked the engine. It had been several seconds since the last gunshot, and Jack had lost sight of the shooter. He could be taking aim, reloading or on the ground by now and headed their way. "How'd you know where to go?" he asked, shifting into gear and craning his neck to check for pedestrians. She'd shoved him off of her and made a beeline for his pickup, a vehicle she'd never seen before. How was that possible?

"What?" Katlin grappled for her seat belt as they lurched into the empty street.

"My truck. How'd you know which was mine?"

Katlin rocked and tipped on the bench beside him as he wheeled around the nearest corner, tires barking and engine roaring.

He dared a glance at her as sirens blared in the distance.

She twisted for a look at the chaos erupting behind them. "You said you had a truck. You said you parked on the street behind the parking deck. This was the only pickup in the direction you were running, and it has a US Army window cling. Your dog tags are hanging from the rearview mirror."

He glanced at the tags and window cling—he barely noticed either these days. "You saw all of that? While being shot at?"

"I guess so." She spun forward and flopped against the seat, pressing a palm to her chest. "Holy cow. I think we can cross off the possibility I was running from a crazy ex, unless I have some seriously awful taste in men."

Jack's lip quirked and a short bark of laughter burst free. "You really are your brother's sister." Griffin had been impossibly calm in every manner of circumstance, right up to the end, when all he'd cared about was that Jack looked after his baby sister and made sure she knew Griffin loved her.

He forced the wedge of emotion from his chest and made a series of quick turns down neighboring streets until he was certain they hadn't been tailed. Then he settled onto the highway to collect his thoughts and make a plan. "I don't suppose being shot at roused any memories?"

She shook her head and rubbed her palms over the tops of her thighs. "Someone tried to kill me last night." The quiver in her voice drew his attention.

He glanced her way, unsure if a memory was resurfacing or if the weight of it all was finally registering.

"Someone didn't just run me off the road in the middle of the night and leave it at that," she said, turning wide brown eyes on him. "They sent a gunman to a hospital to finish me. What the hell did I get into?"

That was what Jack planned to find out.

KATLIN WATCHED THE strangely foreign scenery race by her window as Jack followed Highway 68 west, toward downtown. He'd left a voice mail for a detective once they'd put some distance between themselves and the hospital, then settled into an unnerving silence.

She rubbed sweat-slicked palms against her jeans and hoped she was right to trust him. In a world where she knew no one and had already been shot at, it seemed ridiculous for her to trust anyone, and yet she did.

He took Exit 119 then crawled to a stop at the bottom of the ramp. "This is the exit where the nurses say you crashed. Any idea why you were here?"

Katlin scanned the area. The neighborhood was seedy and run-down with the kind of atmosphere that screamed high crime and low morale. She shook her head. "None of this is familiar. Do I live near here?" If so, what was her life like? Did she run with a rough crowd?

"No." Jack took a left and circled a few blocks, pausing to look both ways at the intersections, his features set in a frown. There were bars on doors and windows. Sneakers hanging from power lines. "Stop me if something rings a bell."

She crossed her arms and rubbed the chill from her skin as irritation crept into her thoughts. Did he think she might regain her memory and not mention it? That she would see someone or something she knew, and just keep it to herself? She furrowed her brow as she stared across the darkened cab. She didn't remember the specifics from her life, but she was certain she hated being treated like someone with a diminished IQ.

She refocused on the sketchy world beyond the window. "Why would I be somewhere like this?" Why would anyone? Nothing good came to mind. "This looks like the sort of place where people go to find drugs or prostitutes."

"Agreed."

"The hospital staff didn't mention any drugs in

my system, and I don't feel like someone dealing with an addiction." In fact, aside from the bumps and bruises, she felt pretty good. Healthy. Fit, even. "I don't think I'd need a prostitute, either," she said, regaining her humor. "People our age just go online or to a bar when they want to hook up, right?"

Jack slowed at the next stop sign and gave her a thorough once-over that sent heat straight to her core. "I don't."

She laughed, a bubble of nervous energy breaking free. "Well, I doubt you have to go searching for a hookup, so you don't count."

Jack turned his eyes back to the road without comment and reentered the highway on an eastbound lane. He leaned forward, scanning the road, and Katlin matched his posture.

Skid marks peppered the pavement, illuminated by the beams of his headlights. The marks were sporadic at first. Then more frequent, growing thicker and darker until they left the road completely, ripping parallel tracks through the scraggy grass beyond the shoulder.

Katlin's stomach tightened with instinctual fear and the phantom sensations of plummeting. Her mind ached to remember the moments her car had left the road and the events immediately before, but the thoughts were locked just outside her reach.

Jack eased onto the road's edge and shifted into Park. "I want to take a look. I'll only be a minute." He activated his emergency flashers, then got out to examine the crash site.

Katlin followed.

The rutted tracks, presumably made by her tires, were visible beneath a path of broken tree limbs over the hill beside the berm. The tracks ended abruptly at the river's edge. Hitting the trees' trunks at highway speeds would have killed her, but she'd hit a network of limbs that had bent and broken, probably saving her life. And they'd kept her from reaching the water, where she would have surely drowned.

Jack pressed broad palms to narrow hips and stared into the early morning. "You should be dead." He shook his head and sighed. "The fact you're standing here, no worse for wear, is a flat-out miracle."

She moved to his side, feeling the truth of that statement in her soul. "That makes twice now. I guess I have a guardian angel."

There was sadness in his eyes as he turned back for the truck and opened the door for her. "I should've called," he said quietly as she climbed inside. "I sent cards, but I should've called. Maybe you wouldn't have come out alone last night, and I could've protected you." He shut the door and rounded the hood, back to his position behind the wheel.

"You're here now," she said. "And I could've called you sooner. You said you put your number in the cards."

He turned his phone over in his hand, unresponsive to her rebuttal, and swiped the screen to life before starting the engine.

"Did we learn anything from the crash site?" she asked. "Besides I'm lucky to be alive?"

"It's still too dark. I'd like to get a look at your

car if you're up for it. Then we'll head over to your place so you can rest."

"I've been out cold since the crash. I'm rested and amped up on adrenaline," she said. "So…"

Jack smiled. "Okay. Let's go see the car first." He set the phone in his cup holder with the GPS app open and merged back onto the highway. "Sun should be up soon. We can circle back to the crash site after you get some real rest in your own bed."

"What about you?" she asked. "When was the last time you slept?"

He grimaced and gripped the back of his neck with one hand. "I don't sleep much."

Katlin bit her lip against a volley of questions and folded her hands to keep them from reaching for him. How could someone look so thigh-clenchingly sexy and be so unfathomably lovable at the same time? Or was that just her head injury talking?

"What?" he asked, flicking his gaze in her direction. "What's that face?"

"Nothing." Katlin redirected her attention to the window at her side. She willed her thoughts to refocus and wondered instead about the kind of car she drove and who she was before she woke in the hospital. Not that it mattered now what she drove. Whatever it was had surely been totaled.

JACK PARKED ACROSS the street from the impound lot, in a more habitable part of town than the crash site. Reputable businesses and homes with fresh-cut lawns and tended flower beds lined the curbs. The police station, courthouse and town hall were only a few parking lots away.

He waited for Katlin outside her door as the sun rose higher on the horizon. "Ready?"

She nodded, and Jack reached for her hand. The electricity that coursed through her at his touch curled her toes inside her sneakers.

He cast a furtive look in her direction as they began to walk, and she couldn't help wondering if he'd felt the delicious charge, too.

According to the posted hours, the lot opened at eight. No one would be there for another hour. Jack stopped at the locked gate and took a look at the security cameras pointed at the street. A warning sign about a guard dog was posted front and center. "Any idea what you drive?" he asked.

"Nope." But the place was thankfully small, with a limited number of impounded vehicles, which would make it easier to identify Katlin's car.

Jack released her hand as they walked the perimeter of a tall chain-link fence. The rectangular guard booth was dark. No dog visible. "This place could use my team's help with security," he said, pausing to evaluate things further. "I'm not sure who *can't* break into this setup."

"Are we breaking in?" she asked.

He laughed, then stiffened.

Katlin's senses went on high alert, seeking the source of Jack's sudden tension.

A low, unidentifiable sound reached her ears.

"Probably the guard dog," she whispered. "Which car do you think is mine?"

He waited a beat before answering. "Something with significant front-end damage. Severely scratched paint from the broken tree limbs and maybe mud-caked tires. Possibly rear corner and bumper damage, as well."

"Wow." Her gut twisted again, responding instinctively to things her mind couldn't recall.

She strained her eyes, scanning the lot for a vehicle that fit the bill. Eventually, a familiar symbol came into view on the rear window of a navy blue sedan two rows away. She raised a hand to point it out, and her heart gave a healthy kick. "Look." Below the US Army symbol, six bold words declared "Proud Sister of a Green Beret."

Jack accessed his phone's flashlight app and pointed it at the car, still bathed in shadows.

Her heart seized at the sight of the damage. The front end was smashed. The windshield broken. The left side aggressively dented from the door to the rear bumper. No wonder she'd been unconscious for so long after the crash. Maybe she really did have a guardian angel.

The beam from Jack's phone landed on the rear window, and a silhouette appeared inside.

The dome light flashed on, and the passenger door swept open. A broad-shouldered figure dressed in black stretched to his feet on the far side of the car.

Jack extinguished the light and reached for Katlin. "That's not good."

She stepped back, bumping against Jack as panic rose in her bones. "That was my car, right? He was in my car?"

The figure raised a gun and took aim before Jack could answer.

"Run." He grabbed her hand and jerked her away from the gunman, back into the street.

They threw themselves into the truck as the first bullet connected with his tailgate.

Chapter Five

"What is happening?" Katlin screamed as the pickup fishtailed away from the gunman. Her heart pounded and her ears rang. Emotion clogged her chest and throat. "Who am I?" The words ripped through her, followed by a sob she hadn't meant to let go. What kind of person had a life like this? *Not a good one*, she thought, hating the parts of her she didn't know.

"Change of plans," Jack said quietly, his breaths quick and audible in the silent cab. "We can't stay at your place with people shooting at you every few minutes. And I need a new vehicle. This one's been seen twice. We need to swap it out, and honestly, the police might want to take it somewhere to process. I think we were hit."

"I know we were hit," Katlin said. "Where are we going? To the police station?"

"No." Jack watched the rearview mirror as he navigated the giant pickup out of town. "I'll call in the gunman and update Detective Reihl again, but we're going to Fortress to regroup."

Katlin deflated against the seat back, hot tears blazing trails over her cheeks unbidden. Her leaden arms and hands were weights at her sides. Her reeling mind brimmed with awful thoughts about who she was before the crash. How had she gotten mixed up with a killer and why? Surely she was smarter than to have made choices that would lead her into a life of crime or the world of criminals. Wasn't she? *Clearly not.* Disappointment mixed with fear in her core and pressed the air from her lungs.

Jack reached for his cell phone. He left another voice mail for the detective, then called the police to report the shooting. Finally, he called someone named Cade and let him know he and Katlin were on the way.

He dropped the phone back into his cup holder and lowered his visor to block the now blinding sun before them. "Cade's meeting us at Fortress. He'll get the coffee on and make up a bunk, where you can rest a few minutes while we set a plan and swap the truck for a company vehicle."

"Is that safe?" she asked. "Trading your personal truck for a company car? What if the shooter got a look at your plates? If he can name you, it won't take long to link you to Fortress," she said, alarm ricocheting through her. "If he looks into Fortress, he'll find the vehicles registered to the company. Then everyone driving one will be in danger."

Jack frowned. "We only drive the fleet as needed, and no one has one out right now, as far as I know. Even if they did, my guys wouldn't be in danger.

Whatever hornet's nest you kicked is no match for them, their training or their fortitude. When I tell you that you're in good hands now, I mean it."

She bit her lip and stifled the urge to point out she'd been shot at twice while in his care. Bottom line, she supposed, was that she hadn't been hit and she probably would have been without Jack at her side. "How long will we stay at Fortress?" she asked. "I don't want my presence to cause anyone else injury." *Or worse.* "Unless Fortress Defense is located on an island, there must be other people nearby, other offices or neighborhood residents who will be in danger if the shooter finds me there."

"We're only staying long enough to form a plan and gather necessities. From there we'll choose a safe house."

Katlin considered his words, attempting to make sense of what would happen next. "So the shooter will track us to a secondary location instead of the office?"

"No." He cast a curious look in her direction. "The shooter isn't going to find us. I'm trying to keep you away from the danger, not bring it to your doorstep."

She huffed. Didn't he know no place was safe in this day and age? "Anyone can do a title search for properties owned by your company and find us. If I'm not at my place when they come for me, they'll go to yours. They can find your address through your truck title. Once they link you to your company, it's an easy jump to assume you're hiding me at another location."

Jack scoffed. "What kind of amateur operation do you think we're running?" Offense dripped from his words and darkened his expression. "It's not like our safe houses are listed in a directory somewhere. The cars and the homes are all owned by an LLC and the link between that dummy corporation and our company is buried pretty deep. It's not impossible to make a connection with time, but we're hoping to get this wrapped up before it comes to that." He stole glances at her as they picked up speed outside town. "This isn't our first rodeo, Katlin. You're going to have to trust us."

She fought a shiver as he rolled her name off his tongue like a caress.

"Worst-case scenario," he said, forcing a small smile, "we leave the country to keep you safe and let my men finish the job. How does Belize sound?"

With Jack? Belize sounded pretty darn good. "You're joking."

He shrugged. "A little. But we will keep you safe. You can count on that."

She inhaled deeply, then released the breath. Jack hadn't failed her yet. And she couldn't do much on her own without her memory. "Okay."

"You ask a lot of deep questions for someone who can't remember their last name."

"It's Andrews." Katlin crossed her arms, then rolled her eyes. "It was printed on all the release papers at the hospital."

Jack barked a laugh. "Smart. Quick. Observant. You're going to be just fine, Andrews."

She could only hope he was right.

JACK PILOTED THE pickup into the underground parking area at Fortress Defense, squinting briefly as his eyes adjusted to the dimmer light. He saluted the security camera as they motored past. The lot was larger than the team needed, easily accommodating staff and guest vehicles, plus the small fleet of company trucks.

"This whole building is yours?" Katlin asked, sitting taller as Jack slid into a spot near the door.

"Yeah." His team had gotten lucky. The company who'd designed and built the building had been foreclosed on, and Wyatt, the one who came up with the idea for Fortress, purchased the place for two-thirds its value. The previous owners had a solid security system already in place: network cables, cameras and receivers. Fortress only had to update and personalize things, then set up shop for business.

He climbed out and headed for Katlin's side of the truck.

She met him there, already closing the passenger door behind her. "I didn't realize you were such a large operation. Do you use the whole building or is there a lot of empty space?"

He smiled. The building was single-story with parking beneath, and Fortress made use of every corner. "There are only four of us now, but we're growing. The waiting area and offices occupy the main space. Aside from that we keep a fully stocked arsenal and extensive equipment lockers. Plus, each team member has a private bunk space for times we're on call or crashing between jobs. And there's a kitchen, gym and shower area." He swiped his key card then tugged open the etched glass door for her. "Bulletproof," he said, rapping his knuckles on the sparkling surface as they entered the underground foyer.

There was a mosaic tile floor, simple gray walls and a large Fortress Defense logo on the central elevator doors. A security camera in the corner tracked their progress as they crossed the room.

Katlin took it all in with a soft "Oohh."

"Like it?" he asked, uncharacteristically tense as he waited for her response.

"Yes. This is impressive." She turned in a small circle, taking in the area, then traced her fingertips over the logo on the shiny elevator doors.

Katlin stepped aboard when the car arrived, and an odd wave of pleasure swept through Jack at her approval.

She turned to face him as he pressed the button, commanding the car upward. She tipped her head back for a direct look at his face. Her brown eyes were warm with sincerity. Her expression was vulnerable, something he got the impression didn't happen to her very often. "I haven't thanked you properly for coming to get me at the hospital," she said. "I'd probably be dead by now if it wasn't for you. You've been kind, patient and heroic. You probably don't hear that enough in your line of work, so I want you to know. I'd also like to thank you for your service. Both things mean a lot to me."

Jack's gut tightened at her words. It'd been a long time since anyone had thanked him for his work. He supposed that was par for the course. He was hired to protect people, so it was expected. Still, knowing all that Katlin was going through, the fact that she'd taken the time between crises to acknowledge him did something to his core. "Thank you."

The doors parted, and Katlin turned away, stepping into the waiting area before him.

"Jack?" Cade's voice boomed through the space as his steady footfalls echoed down the hallway in their direction.

"Yeah. We made it," Jack answered, setting a palm against Katlin's back and steering her toward the couches.

An ensemble of overstuffed seating options was arranged on a carpet in the room's center, with a smattering of side and coffee tables around. Wyatt's and Sawyer's wives had added brightly colored throw pillows to the couches and chairs, then topped the tables with realistic-looking fake flowers. The women had made a weekend of fussing over the space and had even added a selection of flavored coffee creamers to the drink bar. While they were at it, they'd also replaced the plain white disposable cups the men had purchased in bulk with an assortment of colored mugs and napkins.

"Hey." Cade appeared a moment later with a laptop and a smile. "Sorry. I was doing some research in my office." He rocked back on his heels at the sight of Katlin, then flipped his gaze to Jack. "This is Griffin's baby sister?"

"Yep." Jack knew what his teammate was thinking, and jealousy pinched nonsensically in his chest. Katlin was nowhere close to a baby. She looked like a freaking pint-size pinup model, and Jack was supposed to somehow stay as close as possible to her while keeping his thoughts PG-rated. It didn't help that she was kind and confident. Sassy and smart. The perfect combination to steal any man's heart, if Jack's hadn't already been irreparably broken by Cara's death, and the bombshell in question wasn't his best friend's kid sister, whom he'd sworn to protect.

Cade snorted out a laugh, then approached Katlin with one hand extended and a fierce grin on his lips. "I'm Cade Lance. One of Jack's partners. It's nice to meet you. I had the pleasure of meeting your brother briefly several years back. My older brother, Wyatt, another of our partners, knew Griffin from basic training."

Katlin looked to Jack.

Cade quirked an eyebrow. "Did I say something wrong?"

"Nope," Jack said with a sigh. "Katlin has amnesia." He'd saved that detail to share at a time when they weren't running for their lives, and this was the first opportunity since they'd met. "She doesn't remember Griffin, or anything about herself or her life before waking in the hospital last night."

Cade grimaced and rubbed his fingers hard across his brow. "Well, that makes things more complicated." He took a seat on the sofa and rested the laptop on the table. "I guess you should tell me everything you know about what happened, and I'll see what I can do from there."

Katlin lowered herself onto the seat across from Cade and rested her hands in her lap. "To be honest, I'm not even sure about everything that's happened since I woke up in the hospital. Aside from being shot at twice in a matter of hours."

Cade's mouth opened then shut. He leaned forward to rest his elbows on his knees. "Jack?"

Jack started at the beginning. He relayed the missed calls, first from Katlin then the detective, and went from there. He rehashed every detail he could remember, then waited while his partner processed the information.

"All right." Cade nodded thoughtfully. "I'll start by tracking Katlin's life through her social-media accounts and see what I can find. Who are her friends, what she's been up to lately... And with whom. Then I'll see about cracking her passwords so she can close or suspend the accounts. Anything I can find out about her, the shooter can, too. With the accounts closed, the information will still be out there, but it'll take more work to find."

Katlin's knee bobbed wildly as she took in the

explanation. "That buys us more time to figure out who's coming after me before they turn up again. Like getting a replacement truck and staying at a safe house."

"You got it." Cade stretched onto his feet and headed for the hallway again. "I'll be right back. I almost forgot. My fiancée sent some clothes for you. We didn't know your size, so she sent some of those stretchy clothes she jogs in. You've got to be ready to change out of that scrubs top and bloody jeans."

Katlin looked down at herself then cringed.

"You okay?" Jack asked.

"I forgot how awful I look. There's blood on my pants." Her eyes glossed suddenly with unshed tears. "It was really kind of Cade's fiancée to think of me like that," she said. "I hope I was that nice before." She swiped a renegade tear and batted the rest into submission. "Based on everyone wanting to kill me, I'm starting to think I was awful."

Jack crouched into a squat before her. "Hey," he said softly, drawing her eyes to meet his. "The fact you're worried about being awful tells me you weren't." He set a gentle hand over hers and leveled her with his most sincere stare. "You're going to get through this, and you're going to be okay. I won't leave you until I know you're safe and you want me to go. Okay?" And to be honest, he wasn't sure he'd want to go then, either. He traced her porcelain skin with his eyes, noting the feminine lines of her jaw and cheeks, the enticing curve of her neck.

She wet her lips, and Jack allowed himself the

indulgence of trailing the path of her tongue with his heated gaze. He allowed himself one moment to imagine the taste of her smooth pink lips under his.

"Jack," she whispered, the sweet sound tightening his muscles impossibly further. "What if I don't remember?"

He forced himself back to the moment and gave her small hand a light squeeze. "You will. You're smart, and you're strong. Once we clean up and get a little rest at the safe house, we'll visit your apartment. Something there might be exactly what you need to access your memories. And we still need to meet with Detective Reihl. She might have more information we can use, too."

"Okay." Katlin turned her soft hand beneath his, aligning their palms until a jolt of heat and need lanced through him. She spread her fingers, allowing him to slide his between. "Are you sure we've never met?" she asked, searching him with seemingly all-knowing eyes. "Because you feel so familiar."

He agreed. He'd felt it, too.

Cade whistled his way back into the room. "I think this is everything. She sent a bunch of travel-size shower stuff, too."

Katlin released Jack with a blush and a start.

He stood to take the bags from Cade's hands. "Thanks."

Cade smirked, his attention flipping from Jack to Katlin, then back. His smile widened.

Jack moved to the broad reception desk and snagged two sets of keys from the pegboard on the wall. "I think we'll go ahead and get set up at the safe house, then call in and work out an action plan. See what you learn from her social media, and try to get a number where we can reach her folks."

Katlin said goodbye to Cade, then met Jack at the elevator. They stepped inside and watched Cade slowly disappear behind closing doors.

"Good luck," Cade called, a wicked gleam in his eye.

Jack swallowed a groan. He was definitely going to need it.

Chapter Six

Katlin's eyes grew heavy as Jack drove along the scenic country road toward the safe house. The pain medication she'd been administered at the hospital was wearing off, and her aching head and limbs longed for rest. The cab of their new truck was immaculate, had probably been detailed recently. An antiseptic scent of cleansers hung in the air, sharp and uninviting. She much preferred the hints of spearmint and aftershave that had lingered in the fabric of Jack's truck's seats. Otherwise the company truck wasn't bad. Standard size, a few years older than Jack's and in a boring shade of gray. There were no dog tags on the rearview mirror. No window clings spouting army pride. This truck was impersonal and utterly unremarkable. Easy to overlook in a lot or on the road.

The sound of crunching gravel pulled her eyes open sometime later. She hadn't realized she'd let them close. Farmland stretched to the horizon beyond her window. A cloudless blue sky arched overhead.

Jack guided the pickup down a winding lane, pitted and pocked from age and wear, toward an old white farmhouse in the distance.

Katlin straightened to admire the obviously historic home. Detailed scrollwork adorned the window frames and rooflines. A broad wraparound porch and stained-glass transoms showcased the front door. "Wow."

"You like it," Jack said, a note of pride in his voice.

"It's beautiful." The paint was chipping and the flower beds were all overgrown, but the bones of the home were magnificent. The roof was straight and the porches level. "This was probably a mansion in its day."

"It was," Jack said. "The original owner made a mint farming wheat, corn, oats and tobacco. The home was passed down by legacy until there were no more living heirs and it went to sheriff's auction."

Katlin smiled. "And the thrifty, resourceful team at Fortress Defense saw an opportunity to make a deal." She curled her fingers around the door handle, eager to take a closer look. "What's the inside like?"

"Utilitarian," Jack said, parking the truck behind the house. "Clean, dry and stocked with necessities, but very basic. The place isn't used often enough to leave anything of value. Plus, it's a prime location for vagrants or mischievous area teens who might notice no one's living here."

"Security?" she asked.

"No." Jack pocketed the key from the ignition and opened his door. "The monthly fees associated with ongoing service aren't cost-effective. We set up temporary networks as needed then take them down when we leave."

Katlin stretched gingerly onto her feet outside the truck and inhaled the brisk autumn air. Winter was coming. It wouldn't be long now.

"Come on." Jack appeared at her side, the bags from Fortress, plus a couple that had come with the truck, on his shoulder and in his hands. "I think we should get some rest first. Make a plan second, with clear heads. Then go out and look for your memories after we eat." They walked around to the front of the house and headed up the porch steps. Jack slid a key into the dead bolt.

Katlin followed, her stomach groaning at the mention of food. Her limbs, however, begged for sleep.

The front door opened to a small entryway with a staircase to the second floor.

Jack moved into a living area and tossed the black duffel bags onto a couch, then turned an odd expression on her. "How about a quick tour? Then you can clean up or nap, unwind, whatever you need. But there's only one bathroom. We'll have to share while we're here."

"Okay, but how many bedrooms?" She grinned, attempting to be witty, but suddenly regretting the choice.

Jack blanched.

"I didn't mean…of course, we aren't going to…" She motioned between them, then pressed a hand to her mouth in an attempt to shut up.

He turned and left the room, angling his head over one shoulder, indicating she should follow.

The rooms were beautiful but mostly empty and well-worn, like treasures in need of a little polish. Faded wallpaper clung to aged plaster and intricate woodwork lined ceilings, windows and floors.

Narrow beams made up the hardwood floor underfoot, each grooved and stained from wear. The living area had a couch, chair and coffee table. The kitchen had a small four-seat table, coffeepot, stove and refrigerator. The cabinets were tall and spacious, stretching to the ceiling along the far wall. A small hall led to additional rooms and the back porch.

"The parlor and study have been set up as bedrooms on this floor," Jack said, pushing a set of pocket doors wide. "This was the parlor. The study is across the hall. First-floor rooms are easier to defend and easier to exit in the event of an emergency."

Katlin stepped carefully into the room, hyperaware of the gorgeous wrought iron bed against the far wall. Its thick eyelet comforter and a multitude of pillows called to her. The entire setup was reminiscent of another time. For one silly moment, she imagined leading Jack there. If he was half the lover he was the fighter and friend, it'd be a night she wouldn't forget.

Except, she had already forgotten too much, and she was worried about the person she might be. If her suspicions were right, based on what little she had to go on, she wasn't the kind of person Jack deserved.

He cleared his throat and backed out of the room. "The bathroom is this way."

Katlin followed him past an open door to a room across the hall from hers. That room had a simple full-size bed with a plain blanket and a single pillow. Jack's, she assumed.

He flipped the light on inside a large room with a claw-foot tub and freestanding vanity beside a pedestal sink and toilet. "There's aspirin in the cabinet. I'm sure you're feeling the effects of your crash by now." He set the bags Cade's fiancée had provided on a small table in the powder room, then ducked out. "I'll get the perimeter cameras set up," he called, moving quickly out of earshot.

Katlin rubbed her forehead, humiliated by her earlier comment on the number of bedrooms, then locked the bathroom door. The weight of her life pinned her to the wall, and she let her knees buckle, taking her all the way to the floor, where she gave in to the tears.

JACK WHISTLED HIS way around the kitchen the next morning, flipping pancakes and sipping black coffee. He'd gotten three consecutive hours of sleep before dawn, thanks to the well-established security perimeter he'd set before bed. There was a lot to be said for surveillance cameras and a hot spot.

He'd worked into the night attempting to create a narrative for Katlin's precrash life, but he'd come up short on that front. She'd taken impressive measures to control the amount of information available on her personal life, and it had paid off. Something she'd likely learned from her brother, a master of discretion.

As far as Jack could tell, Katlin had one tightly managed Facebook account, and no other social media. Not even a profile on one of those professional networking sites. Her digital footprint was practically nonexistent, and Jack couldn't help wondering what that said about her, or possibly, her career.

Could she be in law enforcement? Maybe undercover?

The sound of her soft footfalls in the hall drew a smile across his mouth. He'd realized he missed her as he'd crawled into bed, thankful there were two rooms where they could sleep. He was only human, after all. "Mornin'," he called, pouring and delivering a fresh mug of coffee to the table. "How are you feeling?"

"Better." She moved into view, a shy smile on her lips. "Apparently Cade's fiancée is pocket-size."

He gave the formfitting black pants and clingy long-sleeve T-shirt an appreciative look. Several parts of him were certain they owed Lyndy a thank-you. "She's petite."

Katlin laughed. Her blond hair hung across her shoulders in waves, curling casually over her breasts and drawing his attention where it didn't belong. "Sorry I fell asleep yesterday. I only meant to rest for a few minutes, then I woke around midnight." She rolled her eyes. "I figured you'd hear me if I got up, and I didn't want to disturb you, so I read the books on the table near my bed and dozed off and on from there."

"You didn't have to stay in bed or worry about disturbing me," he said. "And you can thank Emma for the books. That's Sawyer's wife. She came out here with him this summer when he mowed the grass. She thought the guest room was sad and uninviting, so she tried to improve it."

"It's nice. You should thank her for me the next time you see her." Katlin shuffled to the table, where Jack had set the coffee. "Is this for me?"

"Yeah. And I hope you're hungry. You like pancakes?"

"Yes," she said, groaning the word. "I love pancakes. I could probably eat about twenty of them."

"You remember?" Jack asked, hopeful.

Katlin wrinkled her nose as she sipped her coffee. "No. It's more like an instinct than a memory. Sometimes, when I'm not trying to think of things, they just come to me. Like, I know I love to dance, but I can't actually remember dancing."

"Gotcha," Jack said. "Anything else?"

"Some little things. I'm pretty sure I prefer country music to pop, and would much rather be outside than in."

"Me, too." Jack ferried a heaping platter to the table, then delivered a bottle of syrup with place settings for Katlin and himself. "Help yourself."

Katlin took a pile of pancakes, then greedily dug

in. "Thank you so much for this. I know I'm not pulling my weight yet, but I will."

"You're healing, and you don't need to do anything else. I've got the rest."

"I should be helping." She slid a bite between her inviting lips and let her eyelids flutter in pleasure. "This is delicious. I wonder if I can cook."

"I'm sure," he said. "It's not hard, and you're smart."

"How do you know?" She set aside her fork and raised her eyebrows in challenge.

He sipped his coffee, enjoying the quiet moment with her, happy to share the impressive news. "Griffin came home for your college graduation. I heard about it for weeks afterward. You were at the top of your class."

"Really?" She lifted the fork again, clearly considering the information. "Interesting. Where did I go to college? What was my major?"

Jack stretched his memory, easily recalling the photos on Griffin's wall, but unable to find the details. "I'm not sure."

"Bummer." She pulled her lips to the side. "Hopefully I'll learn more when we get to my apartment."

Jack nodded. "That reminds me. I went over your hospital discharge papers, and I noticed the address there didn't match the one where I've been sending your birthday and Christmas cards. When I spoke with Detective Reihl, she said the information was pulled from your driver's license."

"Probably," Katlin said. "I wasn't awake when the

papers were filled out, but I've looked at the papers and my license. The addresses definitely match."

"Then I guess you've moved." He shrugged. *And Katlin didn't tell him.* He wasn't sure why the fact stung, but it did.

She froze, her fork midway to her lips. "You finally got to speak to the detective? What did she say about the shooters? What did she know about me?"

"Not much." Jack felt his lips pulling low into a frown. In truth, Reihl had been skeptical. She'd made him feel as if he was hiding something or covering for Katlin, though she hadn't said what she thought was going on. "She's as surprised as we are by the gunmen and general chaos that unfolded after your crash. She wanted an address for the safe house, but I told her I'd prefer not to divulge that information yet. When I reminded her that you'd called me instead of 911, implying you had reason not to trust local law enforcement, she relented. But I can't say she'll let it go for long."

Katlin forked another bite of pancake and dragged it through the puddle of syrup on her plate. "There's also the possibility I was involved in criminal activity, and that's the real reason I didn't contact the police."

"I don't think so," Jack said, and though he couldn't say for sure, every instinct he had said Katlin was as honorable and just as she was dangerously tempting.

TWO HOURS LATER, he parked outside a set of apartments in a town thirty minutes from the place he normally sent Katlin's Christmas and birthday cards.

"This is it?" she asked, comparing the address on her license to the building beside them. "Yuck."

He didn't disagree.

"Maybe I did run with criminals," she said. "Because this place isn't much better than the area where I crashed."

Jack met her on the sidewalk as she grimaced at the somewhat run-down apartments. "This neighborhood is about one hundred times better," he said. "This building has just seen better days."

Katlin didn't look convinced as she dug into her purse and retrieved a key ring with lots of options. "Good grief. Why on earth do I have all these?"

Jack smiled. "Let's just hope one of them opens your apartment door."

They moved along the squat brick building to a door marked with the same number as her license, and Katlin tried the keys until one turned the lock. Her shoulders sagged with relief. "Sorry I didn't tell you I moved," she said before turning the knob. "That seems like a rude thing to do."

"To be fair, we'd never met," Jack said, warmed again by her consideration of him when her life was such a mess. "It wasn't as if we were friends." He waited while she opened the door and ushered him inside.

"We should've been," she said. "I think we make great friends."

Jack snorted. "That's probably because you don't know anyone else right now. Normally, I say as little as possible and stay out of everyone's way." This was different. *She* was different, he realized, then quickly pushed away the confusing thought.

Katlin flipped the light switch beside the door and paused to take in the sparsely decorated apartment. "I think the safe house had more furniture than this." She moved tentatively across the worn carpet, scowling her disapproval. "And it was homier, too."

"Maybe you haven't had a chance to settle in and decorate yet," he suggested, understanding her disappointment. He'd looked into the address where he sent the cards, even done a drive-by after his discharge and considered a knock at her door. He'd chickened out and gone home. That address had been a small bungalow with flower boxes at the windows and a rocker on the porch. Small, but postcard-pretty and obviously loved. The apartment where they stood now had a sad desperation about it. And he couldn't help wondering if something bad had happened to initiate her move. Had she lost her job? Been forced to sell her things and downsize?

A small sound broke the silence, and Katlin froze.

Jack set a hand on the gun holstered against his back.

"Tell me I have a cat," she whispered.

Jack gripped her elbow and pulled her behind him. He raised a finger to his lips, then pointed at the door where they'd just entered. He removed his truck key from his pocket and handed it to her.

She bit her bottom lip in hesitation.

A moment later, a small red dot appeared on her forehead.

"Get down!" Jack yelled, yanking her to the floor with him as the front window shattered.

Katlin screamed and covered her head.

His ears rang as he spun and took aim, prepared to fire. "Go!" he hollered, daring a glance at Katlin before making his way to the nearest doorjamb and bracing himself there for cover.

"Come out!" he called into the apartment. "Put your hands up where I can see them. Police are on the way." At least, he hoped that was true. Surely gunfire wasn't so commonplace in the neighborhood that no one had made that call.

Behind him, the front door opened and closed as Katlin found her will to escape. A measure of relief spread through him knowing she had the truck to carry her away if things went south in the next few moments.

"Put your weapon down and kick it out here where I can see it," he yelled. "Now!"

Something thumped against the ground.

Jack's eyes flicked to the object. A remote control, not a gun.

Three rapid-fire shots sent drywall and wood fragments into the air as the doorjamb he was using for cover ripped apart. Jack returned fire, and the front window burst into a confetti shower of glass as the next errant round shattered it. Katlin screamed from somewhere outside, and Jack's heart ripped painfully down the center as he returned fire and told himself she was okay. That she'd screamed at the sound of the gunshots, but hadn't been hit or kidnapped on her way to the truck.

He needed to go after her.

He couldn't go after her.

Not until the gunman was down. Turning his back would only get him killed, and then where would Katlin be? The impossible choice clawed and tore at his chest as he stepped out from hiding and moved methodically through the apartment in search of an intruder.

Until he found an open bathroom window with a trail of blood draped over the sill.

Chapter Seven

Katlin sat at the kitchen table inside her unfamiliar apartment while local police combed through the rooms, dusted for prints and collected a sample of the blood in her bathroom. Her hands trembled with the aftershock of yet another life-threatening scare. She'd been only a few feet away from the front window when a bullet had sent glass shattering into the air behind her. She'd dialed 911 and prayed Jack would be okay. She hated being useless to him while he'd put his life on the line for hers yet again.

Jack paced the space beside her—apparently he was indestructible—and relayed the details of the apartment invasion to someone at Fortress Defense by cell phone. He traded pointed looks with Detective Reihl every minute or two, though the two hadn't spoken since he'd given his initial statement upon her arrival.

Nothing about Katlin's life felt real. Everything was too raw and dangerous. Her heart said this wasn't who she was—not now, anyway. Was it possible to wake up with amnesia and a new personality? Because she couldn't imagine a world where this was really her life. The pathetic, unloved apartment. Only a handful of belongings. No framed photos on the walls or trinkets and snapshots taped to the bedroom mirror. The whole place felt like a larger and more expensive hotel room. Although, even junk hotels made the effort to decorate. Sure, her folks lived overseas, but surely she had friends. Everyone had friends, didn't they? If she did, there was no evidence of them anywhere.

She shot an envious look at Jack's cell phone, then a frustrated look at Detective Reihl, who'd kept Katlin's phone after finding Jack's number dialed immediately before the crash. Tech support was going through it for clues about what happened that night, making the only link to Katlin's personal life locked up in police custody.

The detective moved slowly around the kitchen and living room, scrutinizing everything and frowning often. The pretty brunette had arrived twenty minutes after the initial uniformed responders, looking exhausted and accusatory. She'd gotten the rundown from an officer who'd been dusting Katlin's front door for prints, then taken statements from Katlin and Jack. She'd made it clear she wasn't happy about the number of shootings in her jurisdiction since Katlin's crash, and she gave Katlin the distinct impression it was somehow her fault. Currently, she seemed to be conducting an unwarranted search.

Katlin stood and cleared her throat when the detective reached for a folded American flag in a small display case. "Excuse me."

Detective Reihl lowered her hand, leaving the flag where it was. "Your brother was in the military," she said, tipping her head toward the display. "I'm sorry for your loss."

Katlin raised her chin an inch, wishing she could remember Griffin, and feeling guilty she wasn't saddened by his death. "Have you learned anything about the man who's doing this?"

"We're following every available lead, Miss Andrews." She turned stiffly to face Katlin, head cocked like a puppy trying to understand something new and peculiar. Her gray pantsuit was well-tailored and emphasized a youthful and athletic figure. The tight bun she'd cranked her thick brown locks into seemed to imply she wanted to appear older and more severe. *Occupational requirements for a young female detective*, Katlin supposed.

The detailed train of complicated and somewhat judgmental thoughts stumped Katlin. It wasn't the first time she'd caught herself unwinding an intense line of suspicions and curiosities. Maybe that was what had gotten her into trouble to begin with. Maybe she'd seen or said something she shouldn't have.

Detective Reihl clasped her hands behind her back as she moseyed toward the kitchen. "It would be incredibly helpful if you could remember what you were doing before your crash or anything at all about who might be following you and why."

"No kidding," Katlin groaned.

"Detective?" one of the uniformed officers called

upon approach. He and his partner moved in tandem down the hall, evidence collection materials in hand. "We've got things wrapped up here." He turned to Katlin with a sympathetic expression. "We'll take what we have to the lab and be in touch. You can get a copy of your police reports from the station or online."

Detective Reihl shook the officers' hands. "Thank you both. Let's touch base later."

The men left, and Reihl turned to Katlin, nudging a hunk of destroyed doorjamb with the toe of her shoe. The splintered wedge spun on the floor among bits of drywall debris. She cast a pointed look at the shattered window behind her. "I suggest you stay with family until we figure out what's going on."

"My family isn't in the country," Katlin answered sharply, feeling the well of fear and frustration rise.

"That's right," Reihl said. "Your only known connection is Mr. Hale, a man you've just met."

Katlin bit her tongue to keep from lashing back. The detective was only doing her job, and the situation was unbelievable. Katlin was living it and barely believed it was real—that it wasn't a bizarre dream cooked up in her head while she was lying in bed at the hospital in a coma.

Jack moved into the space at her side, tall, strong and ever-protective. "Something on your mind, Detective?"

"Just making sure I've got your story straight."

Katlin bristled at the implication she might've made everything up. "It's not a story. This is my life, and I'm terrified. You don't think I want to know who I am? Why I live here in this cold, empty apartment? Or why someone wants me dead?"

"Of course," the detective answered. "Like I said—I'm just trying to keep things straight. I can't seem to figure out why you live here, either." She fished a business card from her jacket pocket. "Let me know if that memory of yours makes a reappearance. Or if anyone else takes a shot at you." She passed the card to Katlin, then flashed a tight smile and let herself out.

Katlin fought the urge to scream. "She thinks I'm lying about my amnesia. Probably thinks it's my attempt to hide all the awful things I'm involved in. And what do you think she meant by that comment about not understanding why I live here, either? There was a look in her eye. Like I'm lying about that, too."

Jack moved toward the broken window, watching her leave. "She's run a background check and she has your phone. Maybe she found out you just moved? Your other place was a lot nicer." He turned back with a smile. "You're not some career vagabond. You had a nice little place a couple towns over, and you lived there four years. This place could be nice with some TLC. Maybe you just hadn't gotten to it yet."

She appreciated the continuous encouragement Jack provided, but couldn't quite believe it herself. Something bad was going on here, and she had a feeling it had all started before she moved to this place, especially knowing now that she'd lived somewhere nicer for a long while.

"I got ahold of your landlord," Jack said. "He'll be here to board up the broken window in a bit. He thinks he can get the pane replaced tomorrow. Until then, why don't you pack some things and see if anything personal jars your memory."

Katlin turned on her toes and headed for the bedroom. If she had personal things, the bedroom seemed like the most likely place to keep them. She started with the half-empty closet of too-dressy things. "I can't believe I don't have more clothes than this. I feel like I enjoy and appreciate clothes, but this wardrobe doesn't support that. And most of what's in here is business wear. Am I a businessperson? Because I like the clothes I'm wearing better than any of these, and this outfit isn't even mine." She plucked the comfy T-shirt fabric at her chest. "And if I'm a businessperson, why didn't I rent a nicer place or spend a little money making this one more homey?"

"I don't know, but we will find out. Meanwhile, pack as much as you want. We can take it with us and go through it at the safe house."

She lifted the lid off a box on the floor of her closet and smiled. A small stack of notebooks stood beside a pile of paperbacks. "I knew I liked to read," she said with a nonsensical swell of pride. She had strong reactions to various things and gut instincts about her preferences. That had to be a good sign. Surely the actual memories weren't far behind.

A quick flip through the notebooks revealed nothing obviously relevant or useful, so she moved on to examining her wardrobe.

"Learning anything over there?" Jack called as he poked through the adjacent bathroom.

"Yes. I like to read and prefer running gear to business attire. I'm also apparently completely broke and have terrible taste in apartments and furnishings."

Jack snorted. "We don't know why you moved yet. Maybe this is temporary."

"Yeah," she said smartly, "just until I go to jail for whatever heinous thing I'm involved in."

"That's ridiculous." He crossed into the bedroom and fixed her with a frown. "I might not know you, but I knew Griffin, and he adored you. According to your brother, you are smart, dedicated, hardworking, courageous and loyal, just to name a few of his favorite adjectives. If you were some wayward troublemaker, he would've said so. He didn't sugarcoat things and he didn't lie."

Katlin turned back to her closet and stuffed the most casual clothing options into a suitcase. Then she went to her dresser in search of socks and underthings. Twenty minutes later, she had everything she needed and two boxes of personal items, from miscellaneous photos and notebooks to power cords and an older-model e-reader.

They headed back through the kitchen together, and Katlin grabbed her brother's memorial flag. Her gut said it wasn't right to leave it.

"Do you need this?" Jack asked, lifting a messenger bag off a hook near the refrigerator.

"Maybe." She tucked the flag under her arm and went to see.

The bag was mostly empty and likely used to carry a laptop she hadn't found. She sifted through a collection of plastic cards tucked into one interior pocket. Local library. Gas card. Health care. "Hey." She turned a photo ID over between her fingertips. "Look." She spun the small ID badge so he could see it.

"'Fitch and Quintz, Attorneys-at-Law,'" Jack read the card with a smile. "'Katlin Andrews, administrative assistant.'"

She smiled. "Maybe my coworkers can tell me more about my life than this apartment."

JACK LOADED KATLIN'S things into the truck, then entered her office address into his phone's GPS for directions. She was holding herself together extremely well, all things considered. He wasn't convinced he could do the same in her situation. He had his memories, knew he was a good person and was still darn tired of being shot at. Katlin was trying to piece together who she was with next to nothing to go on, except the fact that a man kept trying to kill her. That had to be an impossible burden.

"Why do you think I live like that?" she asked, eyeballing the run-down building as he eased the truck away from the curb. "Everything about it feels transient and detached. Even the landlord didn't know anything about me, except I pay the rent on time."

The landlord hadn't impressed Jack. He'd covered the window with an attitude, as if it had somehow put him out to have to do his job. He'd had no interest in the break-in, beyond its impact on him, and zero information about Katlin for the police. In fact, the man's line of return questions made Jack suspect he was trying to figure a way to charge Katlin for the damage. Good thing she worked for an attorney.

"You said I have a degree, and I work at a law firm," Katlin continued, "so why does my life seem so lonely and sad?"

"Maybe you're scrimping on rent and general spending to pay down your student-loan debt. That's a real issue for a lot of people."

"Scrimping is one thing. I live like a homeless person. No, actually, I've seen homeless people with more stuff than I had in there."

"So maybe you're a minimalist," he suggested. "One of those new age, vegan hipsters who go around telling everyone to live simply."

She rolled her eyes. "Whoever I am, I'm in a lot of trouble, and I hate thinking I might be a bad person or maybe in debt for more than student loans."

Jack set his hand over hers on the seat between them. "You're not."

She stilled at his touch, and he pulled his hand back, mildly shocked and embarrassed. "Sorry, I didn't mean to…" He let the sentence hang, unsure exactly how to finish the thought. He hadn't meant

to make her uncomfortable. Hadn't meant to over-
step. Hadn't even meant to reach for her. It had been
an automatic response, one he hadn't had in years,
which meant he needed to tighten up.

He fixed his eyes on the road and gave himself a
few swift mental kicks. It didn't matter if he was attracted to her or intrigued by her or even if he felt a
sincere and powerful connection. She was Griffin's
little sister and a client. Kind of. She needed him to
protect her, not touch her at every opportunity.

Katlin set her hand on his, where he'd rested it
on his thigh, then curled her fingers under his palm.

He turned to find a cautious but warm smile on
her pink lips.

She tugged his hand back onto the seat between
them and squeezed. "Tell me about your life," she
said as she watched him intently. His cheeks warmed
as he turned a hesitant smile back to the road. "I
don't know anything about my life. Maybe knowing about yours will help."

"I live alone, like you. I work at Fortress, doing
things like this as needed, though I've been shot at
more in the last two days than I have since leaving
the military. Some days I miss the military," he said,
surprised by the truth in the words. "I liked making
a difference and keeping people safe."

"You're doing that right now," she said softly.

"And I wouldn't change it."

She seemed to consider his answer. "Do you think
you'll ever want a family? Mortgage, white picket
fence and all that instead?"

Jack's heart pinched and his breathing slowed. "I did once." He dared a look at Katlin, hoping to make his stance on relationships clear in case she was thinking about him the way he'd been errantly thinking of her. "She died. Griffin helped me through it, but I don't ever want to go through that again. I wish no one ever had to."

He took the next turn, following the GPS's directions through town, thankful to have said his piece about love. It was a good reminder for his own stupid heart.

"Well, thank you for hanging in with me while I figure things out." She released his hand. "I'm sure Griffin would appreciate it. I certainly do."

Jack gritted his teeth, hating the loss of her gentle touch but knowing it was for the best.

She pulled a bag onto her lap from the floorboards. "I found an e-reader in the nightstand. I'm hoping it has photos or links to my email and social media. If I'm lucky, I kept myself logged in. We can try it out when we're back on Wi-Fi."

"We can use the hot spot on my phone if you want to look while we drive."

She powered the device on and swiped the screen to life, then lifted and dropped her hand. "It has a data plan," she said dryly. "I live like a pauper, but I pay for data on an e-reader. Maybe that's my problem. I'm terrible with money. Maybe the attorneys I work for specialize in bankruptcy."

Jack laughed, glad the awkward moment had passed so quickly. Outside, the sun was brilliant and the day unseasonably warm. A vast and welcome contrast from the day before.

"I have the lamest social-media accounts ever," Katlin scoffed. "It's all generic. There's zero personal information on here. Just memes and famous quotes. Thanks to Griffin, you know more about me than I do. How messed up is that?"

"It's temporary," he said, slowing to the designated reduced speed.

The roads in town were narrow and lined with businesses, from cafés to comic-book shops. Brightly colored flowers and banners decorated light posts and corners. "This looks like a nice little town. People are out walking. The streets are well-maintained. Crime is probably low. Not a bad place to relocate."

She rested her head against the seat back, e-reader in her hands. "Hopefully someone at my office will be able to fill me in on things. They have to be wondering why I haven't shown up at work." Katlin looked his way and frowned.

"What?"

"What if whatever is going on with me has something to do with where I work? It is a law firm. Maybe I'm not a criminal, but I accidentally crossed one."

"Or you might know something you shouldn't."

She barked a humorless laugh. "How ironic. I could be on a hit list for knowing something I can't remember."

Jack cringed internally at the reminder. He slowed at the intersection and engaged his turn signal. "The office is on the next block, so we'll know soon enough. But for the record, I stand by what I said earlier. You're not a criminal. You're a good person. Anyone can see that."

She offered a bland smile. "No offense, but I'll feel more confident about your assessment if I can find a single other person who knows me and doesn't want to kill me."

"Fair enough."

Traffic slowed as they approached their destination. Street congestion created a one-lane situation he couldn't navigate around.

"What's going on?" Katlin asked, sitting straighter and craning her neck for a better view.

"Car accident?" Jack guessed, noting an ambulance and police cruiser along the curb up ahead. He swung the truck into an empty space and cut the engine. "We might as well walk from here. If someone else shoots at us, at least there are already police and paramedics on the scene."

Katlin laughed, and his heart lightened.

He met her on the sidewalk and fed the meter, then double-checked their surroundings for gun-wielding lunatics before turning in the direction of Fitch & Quintz.

Katlin hooked her arm with his and fell easily in step at his side.

They slowed as a line of yellow crime-scene tape came into view, and a uniformed officer exited a building up ahead. He held the door for a pair of

EMTs pushing a gurney into the windy November day. The sheet on top covered a body bag.

The stately gold script on the window behind him read Fitch & Quintz, Attorneys-at-Law.

Chapter Eight

A cold sheen of sweat broke over Katlin's neck and face. Her stomach coiled in silent panic. "What happened?" she croaked, forcing the words through a tightening throat. Whatever it was, she was sure it wasn't accidental—not at her office, not after the last two days she'd had.

Jack set a steady, confident hand over her fingers on his arm, offering his strength. "Excuse me," he called, projecting his voice beyond the caution tape and through the white noise of a gathering crowd.

An officer approached and swept his hands before him, motioning them back. "Please step away from the tape." The man was young and pale with blue eyes and acne. The badge on his coat said Jenkins, and the collar of his shirt was too large for his skinny neck. He barely seemed old enough to be out of high school. How had he passed the service exam? How did she remember police officers took the civil-service exam and not her middle name? She curled her fingers to quell her erratic thoughts and building frustration.

Jack stepped back in silent obedience of the cop's request, towing Katlin with him. "Can you tell me what happened here?" he asked the officer.

"I'm afraid there was a shooting," Officer Jenkins answered. "The law office will be closed today and tomorrow. Appointments will be rescheduled in a day or two."

"Who was shot?" Jack asked.

"That's confidential for the moment. We need to identify the deceased's next of kin before divulging the identity. Now, if you could please step back. Go home. Call and reschedule."

"But…" Katlin croaked, raising her hand and pausing to clear her throat. She forced a calm expression over her face and did her best to appear less panicked and more professional than she felt. With enough luck, the heat creeping over her skin and rolling in her stomach wasn't obvious to everyone who looked at her. "I'm not a client. I work here. I'm an administrative assistant."

The officer lifted his eyebrows. "Is that right?" He removed a small notepad from his interior jacket pocket and turned the pages. "What's your name?"

"Katlin Andrews."

His eyes flicked up from the page, meeting hers with obvious recognition. "Why don't you step inside, Miss Andrews? We're interviewing employees." He returned to the office building and pulled open the door.

Jack cast a questioning look her way, clearly unsure if she was up to being questioned by yet another lawman.

She wasn't. But she wanted answers. "It's okay," she said, nodding and willing her feet into motion.

Officer Jenkins raised a palm to Jack. "Employees only."

Jack looked at Katlin, his hand tightening over hers. There was caution and a measure of fear in his eyes. He clearly didn't like the idea of sending her into the recent murder scene alone. How could she blame him?

"He has to come with me," she told the officer, shoring up her nerve. "He's my personal protection."

Jenkins furrowed his brow.

"Tell him," she whispered, suddenly unsure she could voice all the horrors she'd experienced since waking in the hospital. She met Jack's gaze with pleading eyes.

Jack filled in the officer on the wiki version of events so far, then explained his position with Fortress Defense. "She has a head injury, and her car's at the Campbellsville impound lot. I'm here to keep her safe. I can wait if you'd like, but I can't leave."

The officer looked from Jack to Katlin, then back. "And you're in contact with Detective Reihl about all this?"

Katlin and Jack nodded, and the officer sighed. "All right. Take a seat in the waiting area. I'll be in to speak with you in a few minutes."

Katlin crossed the threshold, mindful of officers and crime-scene personnel passing through the room's center, presumably on their way to and from the location where the body had been found.

The suite was small with a line of uncomfortable-looking wooden benches near the front window. A large oval rug anchored the space between the waiting area and two reception desks—one for each attorney, she presumed. Cherry wainscoting climbed the walls to a matching chair rail, hip-high, and a severe green-and-maroon patterned wallpaper stretched the rest of the way to the ceiling. The lamps and light fixtures were brass. The paintings were landscapes, with gilded frames. Two offices with heavy wooden doors lined the back wall, separated by a narrow hallway and flanked by a sign indicating the way to the restroom.

"Kat?" An older woman with gray hair and pearls approached, clutching the necklace to her breastbone. "There you are. Where have you been? We were worried when you didn't come in or call. And your phone number goes straight to voice mail. We thought you might've quit for some reason."

Katlin worked up a smile—she hated the nickname Kat, and was unsure what to say to the stranger. "Sorry. I was in a car accident and lost my phone. This is the first time I've been able to come in." All true, she told herself, thankful not to have lied to the only person who'd paid any attention to her at the office so far.

The woman gave her a curious look, then belatedly took notice of Jack. "I'm Marsha," she said, offering a small wave. "Kat and I do administrative work here."

Jack smiled cordially, looking impossibly calm and charming in the awful situation. "Jack," he said. "Nice to meet you. So, which attorney do you work for? Or is it a team effort?"

"I work for Mr. Quintz," Marsha said, pressing a wadded tissue to the corner of one eye. She pursed her lips briefly and her eyes darted to Katlin. "Kat worked for Mr. Fitch. He preferred interns over regular full-time employees. It was his way of giving a hand to the next generation. Providing on-the-job experience with excellent credentials for coeds with an interest in law. He was a nice man." Her voice cracked on the final few words, and she moved the tissue from her eye to her nose.

Katlin had a lot of questions about those statements, like why had Marsha called her a coed when she'd been out of college for several years. More importantly, however, was the tense she'd used when speaking of Katlin's boss. "Did you say I *worked* for Mr. Fitch?"

Marsha batted away tears as she tracked the nearest police officers with her gaze. She sniffled, then stepped closer to Katlin. "The cleaning crew found him this morning." She looked at Jack. "They come in at eight and clean before the office opens at nine. The police were here when we all started showing up for work around eight forty-five."

Katlin tightened her grip on Jack's arm. There was no way that was a coincidence. She wondered how long the attorney had been dead. Since Saturday night, when she was run off the road?

Jack moved to a large desk near the window, leaving her to stand with Marsha several feet away.

"Is that your boyfriend?" Marsha asked, peeking discreetly over Katlin's shoulder. "He's very... nice-looking."

Katlin's cheeks warmed at the thought. Silly. Juvenile. Oh, so delightful. "Jack's a close friend."

"I like your desk," he called.

Katlin spun, pulse instantly rising. *Her desk?* Her desk!

He lifted a business card between his fingertips. "Very nice."

"Thanks?" Katlin asked, unsure about his point. Although she admired his steady confidence and the intensity in his eyes, Marsha was wrong. Jack wasn't nice-looking—he was hot and everything about him called to her. Those teasing hazel eyes, the breadth of his strong, broad chest and shoulders, the way he looked at her as if she was a treasure to guard at any price. The way he touched her like it was an honor.

Jack wiggled the card, clearly waiting for something.

"I think he's beckoning you," Marsha said. "But you should tell him we aren't supposed to touch anything."

It took a minute for the words to register through Katlin's muddled thoughts. "Right." She hurried to Jack's side, leaving Marsha to return to the others, a trio in white coveralls. Likely the cleaning crew.

Jack nudged the mouse and Katlin's computer sprang to life.

She immediately took a seat in her office chair.

The air around them was brisk from the open door, scented with old books and new carpet. Outside, Officer Jenkins stood in front of the window. His hands moved quickly as he spoke with the gathered crowd—rubberneckers and lookie-loos.

Katlin set her fingers on the keyboard and willed the password to come to mind. When it didn't, she tried the only things she knew. Her apartment's street number. The birth date on her driver's license. Word and number combinations for everything in sight. The law firm's name. The office address. Nothing worked.

Beside her, Jack poked through the contents of her desk drawers with a pencil. "New-hire paperwork."

Katlin spun in her chair. "Where?"

He tapped the pencil against a set of papers inside her right top drawer.

"I just started three weeks ago," she said, reading the date and doing the mental math. "So I might've moved here for the job. Do you think it's weird Marsha called me a coed four years after I finished college?" Was she changing careers? Why?

"Not really. You look young. Maybe she doesn't know all the facts," Jack suggested.

Katlin set her fingers back on the keyboard and gave the password another try. This time she entered her start date into the password field, and the computer unlocked.

"Nice," Jack whispered, leaning over her shoulder for a closer look.

Katlin double-clicked her office email icon and scrolled through her inbox. Dozens of unread emails awaited. Many were sent from the local courthouse, public defender's office and police station. "How much do you want to bet whoever shot Mr. Fitch was a client?" Katlin whispered.

Jack closed the desk drawer, then pressed his palms on the desk and hovered beside her. "You might've seen or heard something you shouldn't have. Maybe someone wants to be sure you can't repeat it."

Katlin shivered at the thought. Her boss was dead and she would be, too, if it hadn't been for Jack. "We should look into Mr. Fitch. See what kind of cases he normally takes and who his clients are. Anything that can help us figure out what the shooter wants kept quiet."

"Miss Andrews?" Officer Jenkins strode in their direction. His eyes were narrowed and his jaw set. "What are you doing?"

"Checking email," she said, logging out quickly and standing. "I thought I should work until I was questioned. I didn't want to waste time."

"Step away from your desk, please."

She obliged, and Jack followed.

"I spoke with Detective Reihl, and I'd like to ask you a few questions before you go."

Katlin swallowed a groan, steeled her composure and answered his questions without losing her mind or shedding a single tear. Once the officer was satisfied that Jack had told him everything already, she and Jack were free to go.

Katlin fizzed with anticipation as they made their way back to Jack's truck and her e-reader. She'd checked her boring social-media sites earlier, but she hadn't had time to check her personal email before their arrival at the law office. Maybe that was where she kept all her secrets.

JACK NAVIGATED THE truck back through town, keeping close watch on pedestrians and other drivers. It seemed possible the criminal causing all the trouble could be loitering nearby, or at least driving past the murder scene. If not in the hopes of finding Katlin, then to check on the cops and see which direction they were taking the investigation.

Beside him, Katlin had plugged the e-reader into his charger and was sifting through her personal email, which, according to her, was mainly junk. Not the treasure trove of information they'd both been hoping for.

He stretched his memory as he drove, eager for some detail about her life that could spark a memory in her, or at least something she'd be glad to know. She often went to concerts with Griffin and took trips around the world with her parents. Parents that Cade had yet to reach via the only contact number they could come up with. The one Jack had from the year Griffin had died. Katlin had a degree in something and lived in a nice cottage in another town until recently. None of those things were useful to their current situation.

"Wait." Katlin clutched his forearm, and his foot hit the brake.

Katlin rocked forward and the e-reader toppled. Behind him, someone honked. "What are you doing?" she asked, her voice rising an octave.

Jack gently pressed the gas pedal and waved in apology to the driver behind him. "You said to wait. I thought something was wrong. Maybe you saw something outside or needed me to stop or turn back for some reason."

She swiped the e-reader off the floor with a grunt, her hips held firmly in place by the safety belt. "No. I found a link to my monthly bank statement and followed it over to the bank site. So far I've been logged in to all my accounts on this thing. It's brilliant. And guess what's being automatically deducted every month?"

Jack turned curious eyes on her, carefully keeping up with traffic. "What?"

"My utilities. Two sets of them, to be exact. Why am I paying someone else's utilities? And who do they belong to?"

An excellent question. He couldn't think of any reasonable answers and didn't know anyone in her life. "What are the addresses?" he asked, double-checking his rearview mirror before taking the country road that led to the safe house.

"Hang on. I'm not sure if I can access a copy of the bill here." She tapped the screen and scrolled.

"You just started working at the law firm. If you just moved to the apartment, you might still have a final bill for your previous address. That's not uncommon."

"I'm in at the electric company," she said, caught up in her research. "They're charging me for usage at the apartment we visited earlier and someplace out of town. Twelve forty-two Julip Lane, Stanford."

Jack nodded. "That's your last address." He would know. He'd sent cards there for three years.

Katlin made a low humming sound as she continued to tap the screen. "It doesn't say this is my final bill anywhere."

Jack beat his thumbs against the steering wheel, searching for an answer that made sense. "What if you didn't move?" he asked, a new theory taking shape. "It would explain why your apartment didn't look lived in. Maybe it's just a part-time situation, and you still live at the other place, in Pine Hurst."

"Why would I do that?"

Another excellent question. "I'm not sure, but we can drive over there tomorrow and see if I'm right. I'd like to spend the rest of the day following local news coverage on Mr. Fitch's murder and reading up on him and his clientele. The sooner we make a connection between you and one of his clients, associates or friends, the sooner we can put together a possible suspects list for Detective Reihl."

"Okay, I guess," she said. "Better to prioritize naming the killer than worrying about what's going on with my living situation. Hopefully I wasn't living with someone and going through a breakup." She twisted slightly in his direction. "Though that would explain why I moved out and didn't take much with me. Maybe the bulk of the decor and furniture was his. Could that be what happened?"

Jack grimaced. "I hope not." The words were out before he'd thought better of them. "It would suck to leave a place you'd called home with so little of your belongings." Jack refocused on the road, hoping the explanation was enough to make him seem less worried about the possibility she had a boyfriend. "You should see if the e-reader is linked to any cloud storage. Maybe you can access recent photos."

"Good idea." She refocused on the e-reader. "I do," she said a moment later, sounding both surprised and impressed. "And I have a lot of Word documents. Do you think I kept a diary?"

"That would be incredibly helpful," Jack said. "I'm not sure we have that kind of luck."

Katlin was silent for several minutes as they continued back to the safe house.

Jack played a variety of explanatory scenarios in his mind. What did everything they'd learned today mean?

"Jack!" She gripped his arm again, her voice filled with sudden enthusiasm. "These documents aren't diary entries."

"It's okay." He shot an encouraging smile her way. "We'll figure it out."

"No." She shook her head hard and fast. "These files are interviews and news stories." She bit her lip, eyes twinkling. "I'm a reporter!"

Chapter Nine

Jack heated chicken-noodle soup on the stove top and tossed a pair of soon-to-be-toasted cheese sandwiches on the griddle. Now that Katlin had discovered she was a reporter, he could vaguely remember Griffin mentioning her writing. The high-school newspaper. A scholarship-winning essay. Her brother had bragged about her so often, the reasons had begun to blur. And it seemed to Jack she might've been a communications major in college, but he wasn't sure, and she hadn't come across her college details yet.

She was curled on the couch with her e-reader, her back to the armrest, her feet on the cushions, devouring every detail she could find about herself. The small, nearly outdated device was their only link to her life before the hospital, and she was determined to unearth all its secrets.

He'd opted to make lunch while she got lost in the articles and documents on her cloud storage. He'd needed the break from her immediate nearness. After he'd carelessly set his hand on hers in the truck, she'd been reaching for him at every turn, linking their arms and sticking close to his side. It was comfortable, pleasant and deeply maddening.

Jack gave the soup a stir and adjusted the fire beneath his griddle. Did she mean the touches to be so sweet and intimate? Was she growing close to him in a romantic way? Was she bonding with him as if he was a stand-in brother? Surely she didn't cuddle up to everyone as quickly or easily. Did she? And the possibility she'd just broken up with a live-in boyfriend clawed at the back of his mind. How bad must the situation have been to make her leave all her things behind? If the guy existed, Jack wanted answers.

He flipped the sandwiches then swiped his phone screen to redirect his thoughts. He typed the dead lawyer's name into the search engine while the buttered bread slowly turned golden brown. According to the results pages, Mr. Nathan Fitch was a criminal defense attorney. He received his law degree twenty-one years ago from the local university. He was divorced. Two grown kids. A home in a nearby gated community. The handful of news articles where his name appeared were favorable. The bulk of his cases were white-collar and usually dismissed.

"How's lunch coming?" Katlin called, already on her way to his side. Her shiny blond hair fell over her narrow shoulders, and light from the window behind her accented her luscious curves.

Jack set aside his phone, then lifted the corners of his sandwiches with a spatula. "Not long now. I hope you like grilled cheese and chicken-noodle soup. I found bread and soup in the freezer. Butter and cheese in the fridge. Seemed like a no-brainer."

She grinned. "Both sound and smell amazing. It's really kind of you to do this. I can't recall anyone ever cooking for me before."

"Funny," he said, trying not to smile at her joke, and feeling proud of himself for pleasing her. He did his best not to imagine all the other ways he'd like to please her.

Katlin hopped up to sit on the counter beside the stove, her backside just inches from where he'd rested his hand. Her enchanting brown eyes were level with his now. Her feet dangled over the cabinets by his thigh.

Jack's determination to clean up his thoughts weakened, and he instantly imagined reaching for her. Skimming her cheek with his fingertips, gliding the pad of his thumb across her perfect bottom lip before guiding her mouth to his and parting her slender thighs to make room for him between them.

He stepped back, forced his attention to the sandwiches, then removed them from the griddle. He plated the grilled cheeses and ladled soup from the pot, then moved their lunches to the small dinette table. "Did you learn anything new from your files?"

"Yeah. I'm probably biased since the articles came from my brain, even if I can't remember them, but I think I'm a good reporter. The articles were fascinating. I had fun reading them. I might've been a freelancer because I found my byline in a few different papers. Katlin Griffin."

Jack smiled. "A pen name. Interesting." No wonder he hadn't found the articles when he'd searched for details about her online.

"Makes sense if I wanted to maintain some measure of anonymity. Or if I was writing things about people that could've upset them."

"I'm sure you're an excellent and scrupulous reporter," Jack said. "Hopefully a trip to your house tomorrow will restore your memories. I researched your amnesia last night, and most people recover. Occasionally, a trigger will bring it all back. More often it just takes your mind time to relax and let it in. Though, you may never remember every detail of the accident itself. But the rest will come."

The warmth in her eyes softened him, and he longed to pull her close. He shook away the unfair thought. She needed a lot of things right now, but he wasn't one of them. And Griffin would never approve. He'd made that abundantly clear with a thrown punch after Jack had only complimented the photo of a woman he'd assumed was Griffin's date.

He set two places at the table, then looked to Katlin. "The rest of your things should be at the house. We'll get everything we need tomorrow, then let Detective Reihl know what we find."

Katlin hopped off the counter and made her way to the table. "Smart. We can ask my ex-boyfriend all about my life when we get there."

Jack fought the sour expression tugging at his mouth and lost. "Did you learn something from your e-reader about that?" he asked, taking a seat on the chair across from hers and hoping she was joking. His already complicated feelings for her didn't need another kink in the works.

"If I have a boyfriend or an ex, he hasn't reached out via email. Maybe we should go to my other address today. Why wait? Time is obviously of the essence, and I want to know more about myself. I can't understand why I stopped being a reporter. Or why I took the job at the law firm. Was it part of a story I was working on? Was I undercover? Had I been fired? Or did freelance reporting just not pay the bills, so I had to find another source of income?"

"All good questions," Jack said, dunking one corner of his sandwich into the chicken soup. He worried most about her first guess. It made sense that a reporter could find herself in sticky situations from time to time, overstepping boundaries or digging up skeletons better left buried. Research for the juiciest stories had to be tricky. And he could easily see the job at the law firm being a place to access records and eavesdrop, especially given the dead attorney's white-collar-criminal clientele. The scenario was all too plausible, and frankly, he wasn't in any hurry to take her back into the open, where she might be shot at again. Plus, there was plenty of research for him, and healing for her, to be done right where they were. "Let's stay in today," he suggested. "I want to see what we can learn online about Fitch's clients and hear what the evening news reports say on the subject before we head out again. Information is power right now, and we don't have much. We should make our trips short and sweet. Provide whoever's after you with as few opportunities as possible to reach their goal."

Katlin sipped soup from her spoon, apparently considering his suggestion. "Okay. I have plenty of files still to read, and I could probably use the downtime. My head never stops throbbing, and I'm a little tired."

Jack looked more closely at her then, tense with alarm at her admission of physical pain. "Why didn't you say anything?" He hadn't noticed the heavy fatigue hidden behind her smile before, but he should have. Even he was exhausted after the craziness of the past few days, and he hadn't been in a serious car crash. "You should rest. We'll eat, research, make a plan, then start fresh tomorrow armed with all we learn tonight and ready to ask the right questions." Whatever they were.

She bit into her sandwich looking a little unsure. "So you want to just hang out here the rest of the day? And night?" Her cheeks darkened, and her dark eyes flashed. "That sounds…really nice."

Jack worked to keep his mouth from falling open and ignored the painful jolt of desire that pulsed through his chest and into his jeans. There was nothing he wanted more than to protect Katlin, but he was starting to wonder who would protect him from her.

JUST AFTER BREAKFAST the next day, Katlin stood outside an adorable, but unfamiliar, cottage-style home in an inviting section of another town. Jack was still and quiet at her side as she took in the moment. "This is where I've lived for the past four years?"

"Yeah." He cast a curious glance in her direction. "Do you remember it?"

The cold weight of regret pressed against her lungs. "No." Three days had passed since she'd awoken in the hospital not knowing who she was. Each day, her body healed a bit more. She felt a bit stronger and hurt a bit less. But the firm block in her head remained. The frustration was infuriating. The need to relax and wait it out went against her natural inclination to fight and tackle her problems. Regardless of effort, tears and prayer, the memories were beyond her reach and control. Jack had been an incredible comfort to her the night before, when tears of anger and desperation had broken free. He'd held her, encouraged her and made her feel as if she could accomplish anything, even this, no matter how discouraging it seemed. His belief in her helped carry her through the night without another round of vicious self-pity. For that alone, she owed him everything.

"Do you have your key ring?" Jack asked.

She dragged the ring with six keys from her pocket and moved up the porch steps in answer, then tried each key in the dead bolt until one fit. The tumbler rolled and so did her stomach. Hopefully she was right about not having an ex-boyfriend who lived here, but maybe there was a roommate. It would be nice to get details from a person who knew her personally, but not too personally, since she couldn't remember ever being romantically or intimately involved.

The house was dark and silent as they entered. Jack flipped the switch by the door when Katlin drifted past, drawn by intense curiosity and need. She held her breath, listening closely for signs of another intruder, but there was only the pounding of her heart and ticking of a nearby clock.

Jack lifted a palm in warning, indicating she should stay near the door, then walked away. He moved swiftly through the home, clearing the rooms, she realized.

Katlin scanned the inviting space. A warm beige couch and armchair sat on a braided multicolor area rug with matching coffee and end tables. The throw pillows were white with rows of black script across them. She wasn't sure how, but she recognized the text on one as the opening page of *Harry Potter and the Sorcerer's Stone*, another as *Pride and Prejudice*. The entire space smelled like apples and cinnamon, likely a result of the unlit red jar candles on the tables.

"All clear." Jack's strong and level voice registered a moment before he appeared. He rubbed his palms together. "Let's see what we can learn."

A powerful wave of relief washed through her, and her shoulders sagged. Knowing she was safe, having him there with her and loving everything about the unfamiliar home around her, conjured a rock of emotion in her chest. Her eyes stung, and she covered her mouth with one hand as the weight of the moment tried to level her. "I lived here." The words were shaky and the torrent of feelings was nearly too much. "It's charming." She sniffled as she made a slow circuit around the obviously loved and cared-for rooms. There were framed photos on the walls. Stacks of paperbacks on the coffee-table top. And a row of tiny succulent plants in little pots along a windowsill.

She wasn't some half-homeless person living in a run-down apartment without connections to anything.

She was a reporter with a dead boss and weird apartment in the next town.

Tears were replaced with purpose as she moved more quickly through the first floor, trying to make what little she knew add up. There were no boxes or packing materials to suggest she planned to move. The bulk of her things were at this house.

Maybe she'd find her memories here, too.

She paused at the artfully arranged wall of photos, recognizing herself in most, frequently alongside Griffin. He was older in these photos than in the snapshot Jack had pulled from his wallet, but it was undeniably him. The older couple in multiple shots were likely her parents, though she didn't see a strong resemblance. Of the dozen or so framed images, all were of her family.

Family was important to her. She liked that.

She moved on to the kitchen, then stopped as a small table came into view. The two-seater, covered in papers, sat beside a window overlooking the back-yard. And there was a laptop.

A broad smile spread over her face as she approached. The table had obviously been her work space, and whatever she'd been working on was still there, waiting for her.

Jack whistled behind her. "Jackpot." He pulled out the chair nearest to her, and she immediately sat.

She scanned the table, then the room at large, elated and eager. "A cell phone!" She thrust an arm forward, thrilled to see the device on the nearby counter, plugged in to a charger. "This house is magnificent. It's full of gifts, and I never want to leave."

Jack returned her smile. "Understandable, but we shouldn't stay longer than necessary. Just in case we were followed or the shooter figures out you rent this place, too. We can always come back."

A note of sadness tried to find purchase, but bounced instantly away as a new realization dawned. She felt her eyes go wider than her smile. "The phone Detective Reihl has isn't even my real cell phone." She barked a laugh. It probably wasn't very nice of her, but Katlin was glad the presumptuous detective, who'd made her feel as if she might be a criminal, didn't have her main cell phone. Everything about a person's phone was deeply personal. Not intended for anyone, especially local police, to comb through and pass judgment on.

Jack's eyebrows rose. "I guess not."

"Good. I need this one for my memory's sake.

Hopefully there are some recent pictures on it. Maybe those will spark a memory."

Jack plucked the cell phone from the charger and passed it to her. "We can always call and fill her in on whatever we find, if it's relevant to the case. Otherwise, I don't see why she needs this phone. It wasn't part of the crash."

"Thank you." Gratitude filled her, and she stroked the back of his hand where it lingered on the table's edge. When he didn't pull away, she raised her eyes to his and found an intensity there that warmed her in all the best places.

"We can take whatever you want with us and go through it together at the safe house like before."

She returned her attention to the paperwork before her, clearing her throat and doubling down on her focus. A printout from the local college immediately caught her eye. "This looks like a class schedule. Don't I have a degree already?"

He frowned. "Yeah. I saw the pictures."

She turned the paper to face him. "Then why am I registered at Centre College in Danville right now?"

Jack frowned. "The town where you work and have a second apartment." He scrubbed a heavy hand over his impossibly short hair, then rubbed his nicely bearded cheeks in thought. "Taking graduate classes? Maybe the second apartment is just a landing spot for nights when you've been to work and class and can't make it home?"

Katlin considered the suggestion. It seemed financially far-fetched, but who knew? After the last few days she'd had, anything was possible. "The schedule doesn't seem like graduate work, but I'll look into it. Why does every answer lead to more questions?" She tightened her lips against a building tirade. "Nothing makes any sense."

"We're getting there," Jack said. "We have your phone and laptop now. Those should help."

Katlin tidied the papers and folders into a pile, then swiped the phone to life. Her fingertip fit nicely into the small depression on its front, and the phone unlocked.

The thrill of victory whooshed through her as she went for the camera app and flipped eagerly through the snapshots, selfies and candids. She looked so happy in every frame. And she traveled. The couple she'd guessed were her parents appeared in pictures with her in Paris, Zurich and Rome. There were road-trip pics of her and a small redhead with cat-eye sunglasses and ruby lips. Group shots inside a newspaper bullpen. Katlin hiked, biked, camped, skied. Her heart soared and plummeted. She had a full and happy life, and she couldn't remember any of it. Worse, nothing in the camera feed gave a single clue about how she'd gotten mixed up with a killer.

She returned to the phone's home screen, then tapped another social-media icon. She hadn't seen the app on her e-reader. Her home page was basic and showed only a handful of friends and followers, most also students at Centre College.

The messages were short and direct, written across a selfie or snapshot. Katlin flipped through photos of friend groups, shared pizzas, football games and college-campus scenery. One guy's image caught her attention. He showed up more than twice as often as anyone else, and his username was Dylan_242. Blue eyes, shaggy blond hair. A bit of a skater vibe. His preppy clothes didn't support that theory. A rich boy playing at rebel, perhaps.

"Find anything?" Jack asked, striding back into the kitchen.

"I'm not sure. I found a lot of correspondence with this guy on a photo-messaging app." She passed him the phone then stacked the papers on top of her laptop for easier transport. "Give me a few minutes to walk around, then we can head back to the safe house and take our time with all this." She motioned to the stack of materials on the table.

"Or—" he said, his eyes flashing with mischief "—we can visit the newspaper."

He raised one hand into view, a lanyard dangling from his fingertips. The press badge had her photo on it, along with the name Katlin Griffin and the words *Investigative Reporter*.

"I work at the *Covington Gazette*."

Chapter Ten

The *Covington Gazette* was housed in a tall white-washed building beside the local radio station. Like everything else in Katlin's life, nothing about the place felt remotely familiar.

She stared up at the endless windows and shivered against the brisk autumn air. The chill running down her spine seemed appropriate, given she had no idea what awaited her inside. Or if she even still worked there. She rubbed sweat-slicked palms against her jeans and prayed no one would want to shake hands.

Jack beeped the truck doors locked and moved into position at her side. "Ready?"

"Not even a little."

He set his palm against the small of her back, and she felt the zing of electricity to her toes. They moved slowly to the door, and she swiped her badge against the reader. The door buzzed and the lock released.

"I guess you still work here," Jack said.

That was one question answered. They'd discussed a dozen potential scenarios on the drive over, including the possibility that what she was going through had nothing to do with being a reporter, because quite possibly, she wasn't a reporter anymore. The badge could've been old. She might've quit or been fired, then gotten the job at the law office for income. Maybe even decided to go back to school for a degree that more easily translated into a career. Who knew?

Those theories were officially out the window.

They crossed a marble-and-glass foyer to a welcome desk where a woman was on the phone.

Katlin lifted her badge, and the woman motioned them past with barely a glance.

"Tight security," Jack muttered as they climbed the steps to the second floor, following signs for the *Covington Gazette.*

Jack extended a hand to the door at the end of a short hall with the newspaper logo on it. "Here we are."

Katlin swiped her badge over the scanner, and the door unlocked.

Her heart hammered as Jack turned the knob and accompanied her into the office. A bustling world of activity whirled inside. Voices of rushing people rose above the clattering of keyboards and ringing of phones. Cubicles lined the far wall of windows and a center space was made up of simple, interchangeable white desks, each with a chair and monitor. Most were occupied.

Someone barked orders behind a closed office door in the opposite corner, and Katlin's heart raced. "This feels familiar," she whispered, mind humming.

She was almost afraid to say the words, terrified of jinxing the new sensation.

Jack curled his fingers against her back in a move of silent support. "Anything specific?"

"No. Not yet, but it's good. It feels less alien than anyplace else I've been." She pulled in a steadying breath then pointed herself toward a closed door with lots of yelling coming from behind. Instinct told her that was the editor's office. If anyone would know what she was most recently working on, it would be the editor.

"Whoa!" A petite woman with bobbed red hair and glasses rounded a corner. She had earbuds in and a backpack on, but stopped short at the sight of Katlin. She yanked out her earbuds. "Oh, my goodness. You're here!"

Before Katlin could formulate a response, the redhead launched herself across the room at her. She wrapped Katlin in a hug that knocked her back a few paces and required Jack's assistance to keep them upright.

"I can't believe it. I thought you were dead!" She released Katlin suddenly and frowned. "Why haven't you called?"

"Hello," Jack said, flashing a charming smile. "I'm Jack Hale. You must be…"

The newcomer swiped shaky fingertips beneath each eye, ignoring Jack as emotion overtook her. "I was so worried about you. I thought something awful might've happened. I gave you seventy-two hours. I planned to call the cops and report you missing tonight."

"Sorry," Katlin said.

The redhead cast a curious, but fleeting, look at Jack, then refocused on Katlin. "Who's this guy?"

"Jack," he repeated. He extended a hand. "Nice to meet you…" He trailed off, waiting for the redhead's name.

"Maggie. I work with Katlin. She's my best friend."

Jack brightened his smile. "Great. You must know a lot about her."

"I do. She's like a sister to me. How do you know Katlin?" She folded her arms and examined Jack more carefully.

"I'm a friend of the family," Jack answered. "She's showing me around while I'm in town. Did you two ladies meet at work?"

Katlin chewed her lip. She didn't like thinking of Jack as a simple friend of the family when he was so much more, but how could she define it all? And why did it matter? She gave herself a mental shove back to the moment.

"We went to Plymouth together, both majored in communications and got internships here after graduation. We've known each other for years." She swung her gaze back to Katlin. "Which is why I can't believe you haven't called. I've been sick. I haven't eaten in two days. I lost three pounds. Thank you for that last part, but all the rest sucks."

Katlin laughed. It was easy to see how she and Maggie had been friends.

"Did you get the story?" Maggie asked, her small frame going still. "At least tell me whatever you were up to was worth it, and that there's an excellent reason you scared me half to death."

Katlin shifted her gaze to Jack, unsure how much she could tell Maggie. Could she be trusted? If so, would telling her put her in danger?

"You say you're like sisters?" Jack asked Maggie.

"Sure," she said, a mischievous smile on her lips. "Family's not always blood, you know?"

"I do." He locked eyes with Katlin and gave a nearly imperceptible nod. "Is there somewhere more private where we can talk, Maggie?"

Maggie frowned. "I guess." She looked to Katlin.

"Please," Katlin said.

Maggie turned and headed for an empty cubicle near the window. The neighboring unit was empty, as well, and the man at the nearest desk wore headphones. Maggie hopped onto the desk and sat on a giant paper calendar, dangling her feet over the drawers. She motioned for Katlin to take the office chair. "What's up?"

"I have amnesia," Katlin said, jumping into what was sure to be a confusing and bizarre conversation.

Five minutes later, she'd shared all the key points of her nightmare, and Maggie stared back, agape.

"So you really don't remember anything?"

Katlin shook her head, nonsensically ashamed. She'd researched cases of memory loss like hers over the last two days and knew she was likely to blame. Specialists believed patients intentionally blocked things they couldn't deal with. In Katlin's book, that equated to cowardice. It wasn't just her life on the line anymore. Jack was right there with her, and her subconscious still chose to protect itself over him. Was she so emotionally delicate she couldn't face reality? Was this kind of thing typical of her? Her stomach sank at the thought. It wasn't who she wanted to be.

"Nothing?" Maggie asked, sweeping a hand meaningful between them. "Your work? Your past? Your family? Me?"

"I'm sorry."

Maggie hopped off the desk and closed the space between them, then wrapped her arms around Katlin. "That must be so awful. I wish I could fix it."

Jack cleared his throat. "Maybe you can help."

Maggie released Katlin, a hopeful look in her eyes. "Anything. Name it."

"Tell us whatever you can. About her life. The story she's working on. Anything. Maybe something will trigger her memories," he suggested. "Or at least help us figure out who's been trying to kill her."

Maggie's expression was aghast before she looked suddenly delighted. "Come with me."

She led the way around the shared cubicle wall to the empty unit beside hers. "This is your desk."

Snapshots of Katlin and Maggie hung on the padded walls. "I have this one on my phone," Katlin said, pointing to a selfie of her and Maggie on a road trip. Photos of a man in his dress uniform, she recognized as her brother, and others of her with him on mountaintops and at concerts, littered the space above her monitor. She touched the corner of one image, wishing with all her heart to remember.

"You were working on a story about the upcropping of gambling rings near local college campuses," Maggie said. "You did a lot of the general research here. You can probably check the history on this computer and read up on the information you started with."

Katlin took a seat and booted up the computer, thrilled with the salacious detail. "College gambling rings," she mused. "That explains why I'm registered for classes when I already have a degree, and why I have a second, barely furnished apartment in the next town."

Jack moved in beside her chair and crossed his arms. "What else can you tell us?" he asked Maggie.

"About the case? Not a lot. About Katlin? Everything."

Katlin groaned at first sight of the log-in screen. "Any chance you know my password?"

Maggie lifted the desk phone and pressed a few numbers. "No, but I know how to get it." She winked. "Hey, it's Maggie at the *Gazette*," she explained into the receiver. "Katlin forgot her password. Great. Thanks!" She hung up and grinned. "Toby's our IT guy. He likes me. He's in the middle of something for someone else, but he's going to reset your password in a minute and call back to let us know it's done."

"Nice." Katlin gave her friend a high five. Meanwhile, she could go through her desk for clues. "Let's see what I keep in here."

Maggie pulled a photo off the wall. Griffin and a group of others in fatigues. "Is this you?" she asked, passing the picture to Jack.

Katlin turned to wait for his answer.

Emotion raced across his face and disappeared before Katlin could name it. "Yes. Griffin was my best friend."

Maggie's jaw dropped. "So, you're The Jack?" she asked, eyes wide. "Like Jack-Jack?"

"Yes?"

Maggie pursed her lips, but a little smile broke through. "Holy wow, and I suppose you don't remember him, either?" she asked Katlin.

"I just met him after the car crash," Katlin said, suddenly wondering if Jack had lied about that for some reason.

Maggie laughed. "Maybe not, but you're crazy about him. You talk about him all the time. He sends you cards every year on Christmas and your birthday, and he always leaves his phone number." She pressed her hands to her chest. "It's the sweetest thing ever, and you love it." She leaned closer to Katlin's ear and lowered her voice. "You saw him at Griffin's ceremony for something or other the year we met, and thought he was the dreamiest. You asked Griffin about him all the time, and Griffin hated it. You loved getting him going, so you teased him mercilessly about coming to visit him so you could get to know Jack better."

Jack chuckled.

Katlin's cheeks flamed hot. She sat taller and changed the subject. "I found a laptop at my house, but it's locked. I don't suppose I could bring that in here and have your friend in IT take a look?"

Maggie frowned. "No. They're always busy down there with help-desk stuff. And I don't know him well enough to ask him to look at it after hours. Did you try Griffin's birthday? You use that a lot. Or the number from his Green Beret group. Troop?" She turned her attention to Jack. "Platoon?"

Jack tugged the sleeve of his thermal shirt over one elbow and up his biceps. "This number?"

Katlin tried not to swoon. New personal discovery. She liked strong, muscled arms. And she loved that ink. "Thanks."

The desk phone rang, and Katlin jumped.

Maggie snagged the receiver off the cradle. "This is Maggie. Thanks!" She hung up and typed six zeros into the prompt on Katlin's screen. "He said to change it once you're in."

Katlin pressed Enter, and the screen unlocked. She quickly changed the password and began to search her mail and files.

"Did you find the Green Beret thumb drive?" Maggie asked. "Your story's probably on there. You were tight-lipped last week about progress, but you said it was getting really big. I guess you were right." Her voice grew sad on the final sentence. "I can't believe you were out getting amnesia and shot at, and I had no idea. I'm a terrible friend."

Katlin lifted a hand. "I'm sure that's not true. I didn't know to look for a thumb drive. Where do I keep it?"

"Around your neck on a chain usually," Maggie said, her gaze dropping to Katlin's chest. "Your brother sent it to you. You guarded it with your life. You have to remember the thumb drive."

"I remember nothing," Katlin grumbled.

Maggie rubbed her back. "Sorry. It's just so weird."

"It's okay," Katlin said. Maggie was right. Amnesia was weird. "If I normally wore the thumb drive on a chain, I wonder if it could've fallen off in the car." She looked to Jack. "We should call Detective Reihl, and maybe check with the hospital." She sighed. "That's all going to take forever. Plus, we'll have to search two residences, and it's probably small enough to be almost anywhere."

Jack pulled his cell phone from his back pocket. "Hopefully that wasn't what the intruder was looking for when we interrupted him at the impound lot and again at your secondary apartment."

Maggie sighed, drawing Katlin's attention. "I hate that you're going through all this alone. What else can I do?"

Jack moved to the far corner of the little workspace and turned away as he pressed the cell phone against one ear. "Detective Reihl, please. This is Jack Hale."

"I'm not alone, and you're already helping," Katlin told Maggie. She pulled the cell phone from her bag and used her fingerprint to unlock it, then swiped to the photo-messaging app. "Now that I know I was looking into a college gambling ring, it makes sense that I'm registered for classes at Centre College. It also explains why I got a job and an apartment in Danville. I created a total cover." The story must've been truly huge to go through all that.

Katlin flipped to one of the many photos of Dylan_242, then turned the phone to Maggie. "Any idea who this is?"

Maggie smiled. "That's Dylan. You've been getting close to him because he's connected to the gambling somehow. He's invited you out for coffee a couple times, but you're still waiting for an invitation to play. You should open the message."

Katlin turned the phone back. A small icon indicated a new message. "That wasn't there before." She clicked the message with bated breath. Did Dylan know who she was and what she'd been up to? Was he the one who'd run her off the road? The one who'd shot at her?

The photo message that opened wasn't of Dylan, it was a snapshot of the river at night with a strange invitation written on the image. "He wants me to take the boat out with him tonight." Katlin wrinkled her nose. "It says the dress is black tie and I should tell the captain I can swim."

Maggie squeaked. "'Take the boat out' is code for their underground casino nights!"

"And the captain is what?" she asked. "The doorman?"

Maggie raised her shoulders to her ears, still smiling. "Maybe? Are you going to go?"

Jack tucked the phone back into his pocket and returned to her side. "No."

His low, authoritative voice mixed with her much higher one as she declared, "Absolutely."

Chapter Eleven

Katlin chewed her bottom lip. The prospect of attending an underground gambling night was terrifying, but if it meant understanding what she'd gotten herself into and who was trying to kill her, she had to check it out. At least she wouldn't be alone. She had Jack, and he had an entire team of former military men on his side.

She scrutinized her reflection in the safe-house mirror, hoping she'd chosen the right look for the night. Jack hadn't been much help. He'd taken her back to her place to find a dress, clutch and heels, but he'd been too distracted making plans with his teammates by phone to help her choose. He'd continued organizing with the team when they'd visited Fortress for his suit and tie. At least Katlin and Jack wouldn't be alone tonight, whatever happened, and she was immensely thankful for that. Two of the teammates were already on their way to set up surveillance outside the venue now, before anyone else arrived. By the time the party got started, all signs of the Fortress men would have vanished into the landscape.

Katlin sighed and twisted in front of the mirror as light reflected off the beads and sequins of her black cocktail dress. The material hugged her body, emphasizing all her curves, then stopped midthigh. The plunging V in back nearly reached her tailbone. Thankfully, the neckline was higher, lying modestly across her collarbone. Still, there was no way to wear anything comfortable underneath. She'd found adhesive bra cups and a barely there pair of panties among her lingerie. So far the pieces were all working, but only time would tell.

She'd had more fun than she'd expected putting on her makeup and was surprised to find she was good at it. The routine of liquid eyeliner, powder and lipstick was comfortable and familiar, as was the process of blowing out her hair and securing it into a neat chignon.

She turned at the sound of steady footfalls in the hall outside her room. A moment later, Jack appeared. He was stunning in a perfectly tailored black suit and tie. His shoulders seemed impossibly broader, his waist more narrow. He'd shaved the small amount of hair on his head and tidied his beard for the occasion. Her fingers curled at her sides, desperate to touch him.

"Wow." He moved slowly into the room, his gaze darkening as it slid over her from head to heels. When his sharp hazel eyes flashed back to hers, there was heat there she hadn't seen before.

"Too much?" she asked, turning back to the mirror and selecting a pair of simple gold hoop earrings.

He whistled long and slow behind her, and she caught his gaze in the mirror as it returned from trailing over the deeply revealing back of her dress. "You look stunning."

"Thanks." She secured the second hoop earring, then turned to face him, admiring his strong square jaw and kind eyes. It was easy to imagine that he was hers, and they were off to a night on the town, a friend's wedding or other normal celebration. One where he would hold her close and she could pull his mouth to hers, kiss him tenderly and often. "This could be it," she said, feeling both hopeful and afraid. Tonight's outing could hold the keys to all her secrets and end the reign of terror on her life. Tonight's outing could change everything. "We might get all our answers at this event." Much as she wanted that to be true, she still didn't have her memories, which left her vulnerable and unsure how to pick up with a life she couldn't recall. More than that, she wasn't ready to say goodbye to Jack. Would he leave her when the job was done?

"We can hope," he said. "My team's in place, so we can go whenever you're ready. My guys will have eyes on the venue's outside and be listening through a microphone on my lapel. If anything goes awry, they can call 911 and get help to us in minutes. In the event of an emergency, they'll beat first responders to our aid. Hopefully it turns out to be an uneventful night, and we can fill in Detective Reihl on whatever we learn tomorrow morning."

Katlin took a steadying breath and nodded. She'd called Jack, a virtual stranger, while being run off the highway, not the police. That had to mean something, so she wasn't ready to just give the address of the event to authorities and hope for the best. Not until there was an officer she trusted as much as she trusted Jack, and that night wasn't tonight. She lifted her chin and tucked her clutch under one arm. "We shouldn't keep the team waiting."

Forty minutes later, Katlin climbed out of Jack's truck at the docks and shivered against the cool autumn breeze.

Jack met her at the front bumper and reached for her hand. "Try to relax," he whispered.

She nodded, feigning calm until her teeth began to chatter.

The air off the water felt like ice on her exposed skin. And the faint scent of brine and decay lingered forlornly in the air. Water lapped lazily against the docks, where a dozen cars and trucks were lined up in the shadows, including, she noted, one ratty-looking unmarked van. Presumably containing the Fortress team.

"Were you able to reach your parents?" Jack asked.

She shook her head, fighting nerves and trying not to chew her lip and ruin her lipstick. "I know parents would want to know what's happening, but I don't remember them. Every time I started to dial the number in my contacts, I hung up before hitting Call."

"Do you want me to call?" he asked, brow furrowed in concern. For her? For her folks? She couldn't be sure, but loved that even in this small task of contacting her parents, he was willing to be her hero.

"No." She smiled. "I'll do it." Just not tonight. She took a step forward, and Jack joined her, setting a warm hand against the exposed small of her back.

He leaned in close as they moved toward the only visible door on the nearby building. "Someone is likely watching the area, so we need to look like a happy couple on a date." His breath blew softly over her ear, sending shivers down her spine and causing heat to pool in her core.

He grazed his lips against her temple. "Now smile as if I'm the only man you ever want to take you home." The featherlight caress curled her toes in the black stiletto heels and a small moan dropped from her lips.

Her eyelids drifted shut to absorb every ounce of the moment.

The low bleating of a boat horn made her open her eyes, reminding her that this wasn't a date. It was a reconnaissance mission in the industrialized section of the docks. And finding the man who was after her was literally a life-or-death assignment.

A man in a black suit, shirt and tie opened the door as they arrived. Someone had been watching,

Katlin realized, and her stomach coiled tight with paranoia.

"This is a private party," he said sternly, widening his stance and glaring at Jack.

"We're aware," Katlin said, forcing a frown and air of pretension she didn't feel. "I'm an excellent swimmer."

The man's scowl relented with recognition of the strange password. He raked his narrowed gaze over Jack, then stepped aside to let them pass. "Have a nice night."

Katlin clutched Jack's arm as they moved down a dark hallway into another world. The sounds of chatter, laughter and the shuffling of cards could be heard behind a dark curtain several yards away. The clanking of chips and glasses played the score.

Another man in a dark suit parted the curtain as they arrived, and he ushered them inside.

Mile-high ceilings soared overhead in the abandoned factory. On the floor, a perimeter of temporary walls had been set up.

Dozens of people filled the space that was ringed with gaming machines and makeshift bars. Multiple green-felt tables with serious-looking card players occupied the center. Roulette wheels spun between blackjack and poker tables with onlookers lingering at every turn.

Jack wrapped a protective arm around Katlin's back. "Not quite the outfit of craps and beer pong I'd anticipated for a college gambling ring," he whispered.

A size-zero waitress in a slinky black gown stopped before them with a tray of drinks. "Champagne? Scotch?"

Katlin drained a champagne flute, then returned it and selected a second. She gave an apologetic smile to Jack. "Sorry."

His lips curved up in a grin. "Better?"

"A little." She wet her lips and concentrated on breathing. "I don't know how to gamble, and I really want to kick the former version of me who dragged me into this." She cringed. "That didn't even make any sense."

"It did," he assured her, curving his fingers against her side. "We'll get this sorted, then you can do yourself a favor and chase leads on community do-gooders and adopt-a-pet events."

"Deal," she said. "But I'm not sure what I'm supposed to be doing here and now."

"Just keep your chin up and your eyes open," he said. "Let that dress do the rest."

She wasn't sure what that meant, exactly, but she liked the look in his eyes when he said it.

They made a sweep of the room, discussed their gaming options and provided his listening teammates with a general layout of the place, just as they'd talked about in the truck.

They stepped apart when Jack spotted Dylan. Jack turned to watch another game while Katlin waved to the stranger and hoped she could make him believe she remembered him. Or anything.

It only took a moment before Dylan noticed her.

He wound his way through the crowd, drink in hand. "You made it." He stopped to kiss her cheek, then checked her out. "Hot damn. That dress is smoking." He ogled a bit longer, and she struggled not to cross her arms over her chest. "No one will be able to concentrate with you here. I might be in trouble." He laughed. "I've got a few losses of my own to recoup."

Katlin smiled back warmly. "Thanks for the invitation. This is wild."

"It is." He sipped his drink, head bobbing as his gaze made a jumpy circuit around the room. A small tremor in his hand belied his cool demeanor. "These parties are a good time until you're losing."

She felt an icy stab of terror on his behalf. Owing money to this group wasn't good. She'd crossed them somehow and they were out to kill her. "I'm not much of a gambler," she admitted, "and I'm pretty broke."

"Don't worry about it," he said. "You're doing me a solid by coming. They like it when we can get women who look like you to stop by. The big fish enjoy the company and admiration. Then they come back. Maybe I can catch a break if they know I invited you."

Katlin stiffened. "I don't understand."

He nodded to a line of older men at the blackjack table. "They feel younger, surrounded by people our age, and it feeds their egos to show off with gorgeous women around to watch."

"Oh." She relaxed into a playful laugh. "Funny. And I assumed this was just a Centre party."

"Not even close." Dylan set his empty glass on a passing server's tray and swiped a full one.

The feeling of being watched returned to her and she fought to keep her smile in place. She hadn't just stumbled onto a thriving college gambling circuit. This was a massive operation, and she'd clearly been in so far over her head, she couldn't see up. Fear and regret for her former self twisted through her. She must've been completely terrified when she'd realized. Must've felt so alone. No wonder she hadn't shared any details with Maggie. Knowing would've put her in danger, too.

But why hadn't she called the police? The question scratched again at the back of her mind. Had she been waiting for an invitation like the one she had tonight? Was the plan to get the location of the next party, then send officers in to raid it? Was that what she should be doing right now?

Dylan's voice faded into the background as she searched for the cause of her growing internal panic. A few men raised their drinks and winked as she met their eyes, but they quickly turned back to their games. Bouncers barely noticed her. Waitresses didn't seem to see her at all.

And then she saw him.

A man in his thirties stood at attention near the edge of the space. His face was unfamiliar, but his stance and frame were burned into her mind. Instinctual fear clutched her heart and demanded that she move. Demanded that this was the shooter who'd come for her so many times already. "Excuse me," she said, cutting off Dylan from whatever he was saying. "I'm sorry. It's a little warm in here and I haven't eaten today. I'm going to get some air."

Dylan smiled, clearly unoffended by her interruption. "Finish your drink," he said. "I'll grab you some fruit from the bar." He turned away, and Katlin spun in search of Jack.

"I'm right here," he said, already reaching for her. "What's wrong?"

"I think the shooter's here, and I think he recognized me."

Jack's posture was tight as he scanned the room. He pulled Katlin into his arms and moving her toward the door. "Blue eyes, salt-and-pepper hair?" he asked.

"Yes."

"Got him. Let's move out. You guys getting this?" he asked, pressing a finger to his lapel.

Katlin craned her neck for a look behind them, praying she was wrong. "He's coming," she whispered.

"Keep smiling and moving toward the door," Jack said. "Once we're outside my men will offer cover. Any sign of trouble, and the police will be on their way."

Katlin's breaths came impossibly faster as they reached the door and bypassed the man she'd given her password to.

"Stop!" a deep voice bellowed as their feet hit the dark pavement and they launched into a sprint.

She dared a look behind her, and found the shooter, widening his stance and sliding a hand inside his jacket.

"Gun!"

Chapter Twelve

Adrenaline spiked in Jack's veins. Katlin's scream registered at nearly the same moment as the gunshot. "Run!" He gripped her hand as they dashed across the parking area, darting between cars for cover, past stacks of abandoned railroad ties and derelict dinghies.

Katlin shrieked and ducked as a second shot rang out, covering her head with her free hand and stumbling on her heels.

"Keep moving!" Jack called. He understood her instinct to take cover, but the truth was that once the shot was heard, it was too late to get out of the way. All they could do was keep moving and hope his team got their backsides in gear.

Katlin rallied, matching his pace, despite the constricting dress and ice-pick heels.

Several yards away, a set of headlights flashed on, and the silhouette of a van peeled away from the other vehicles. Its engine growled as it sped toward them.

"Your team!" Katlin cried, relief and joy in her breathless tone.

A third shot exploded the window of a nearby car, staunching her joy and making her fumble over her feet. Katlin screamed once more, this time going down on one knee.

The damaged car's alarm rang out, its lights flashing, and voices erupted behind them. Gamblers rushed from the building to see what was happening.

Jack scooped Katlin onto her feet when she didn't stand quickly. "Are you hurt?" She hadn't been shot. The bullet had hit a car several yards to the left.

"My heel broke!" she seethed, her voice feral as the van tore past them in the night.

The tires squealed as his team changed directions, rocking wildly to avoid them.

Jack used the fob to unlock his truck doors, and Katlin dove inside. Jack joined her, gunning the engine to life as the sound of gunshots continued. Muzzle blasts lit the night as he wheeled the truck away from the scene—he hoped none of the gamblers or staff were injured in the cross fire.

Other vehicles quickly joined them in their escape, headlights bobbing and weaving in his rearview mirror.

Katlin rocked on the seat beside him, struggling with her seat belt and angling for a look behind them. "Someone's firing on the van," she cried. "Everyone's leaving the building. What if someone's hurt because of me?"

"My priority is you." Jack pressed the gas with

more purpose, needing to put as much distance as possible between Katlin and the danger. His team could hold their own, and they'd likely called the police at the first sight of the gun.

Seconds later sirens wailed in the distance, and Jack relaxed by a fraction. When the emergency crews and police cruisers tore past them, clearly on their way to the docks, he took his first deep breath of the night.

Katlin doubled over.

"Hey." He gripped her bicep, pulling her upright. "What's wrong?" He scanned her small body for signs of blood or injury. "Everything's going to be okay. My guys are well-trained and the police will be there any minute."

Katlin turned wide, tear-filled eyes on him. Her cheeks were scarlet, her lips quivering. She had one high heel in her hand and slammed it against the floorboards. She bent forward again, levering the other shoe off while she cursed and Jack processed the complaint.

He'd been sure she'd passed out beside him, but she'd been taking off her broken shoe? She wasn't sick with distress or limp with fear? She was mad at her broken heel? A small chuckle broke across his lips. "I don't think those particular shoes were meant for evening sprints over concrete."

She glared in his direction, blinking in and out of sight as streetlights passed over them, casting her in occasional darkness. "That was no college gambling ring," she griped, ignoring his comment. "What the hell did I get involved in? There was big money in there. Armed guards. Who apparently have no problem shooting at their guests."

Jack worked to loosen his grip on the steering wheel, then changed lanes and headed for the next road out of town. "Hopefully the team got some photos of the people going in and out. Maybe the shootings haven't been about the gambling itself."

"Like maybe someone important gambles with this group, and I got the scoop that could ruin him or her?" she asked. She'd said something similar to him while looking at all the clearly affluent middle-aged men at the card tables. A ragged sigh escaped her, and she flopped heavily against the seat back. "Why do I chase stories like this? Why put myself in danger? For what?" she asked. "Nothing. And I'm sorry if it offends the woman I once was, but I don't want to be a reporter anymore. I want to get answers for the police on this case only, regain my memories as soon as possible and be done with all of this nonsense. It's crazy!" She swiped tears from her cheeks, looking more angry than sad.

He glanced between her and the road, unsure how to respond, or if she was in shock.

His phone buzzed, and he pulled it from his pocket, thankful for an excuse not to say the wrong thing and potentially meet the business end of her broken shoe. "Hale." He listened as Wyatt gave him a rundown on the situation at the docks, then hung up to relay the details to Katlin, who'd turned to stare out her window.

"Wyatt says everyone got out of there before police arrived. There was a mass exodus when the shooting began. The shooter went back into the building, but didn't come out, and the cops said the building was empty."

"Empty?" Katlin's face reddened. Her jaw set.

He reached for her hand on the seat between them and discovered a clenched fist. "Hey, breathe. We knew this wasn't an amateur operation. They cleared the people as soon as shots were fired and were probably already tearing down the casino as they fled. There were enough men and women staffing the event to accomplish a lot in a short time if they hustled."

She hacked a deep, throaty sound of disgust. "Hustled? They probably run drills for practice."

"Probably," he agreed. "You want to talk about all this yet?" He ran the pad of his thumb over the back of her hand, working to relax her fist. "I'm an excellent listener."

She rolled her eyes. "I'm angry and scared and about a dozen other things I can't even put names to, but mostly I want to slap myself for choosing this life. I don't want to be in danger or on the run like this. I should've turned everything I knew about the gambling over to the police and let them sort it. Instead, I probably wanted the glory for breaking some big undercover story, and look at all the trouble I caused. Mr. Fitch is dead because of my need to get this byline."

"You don't know that," Jack said, feeling a strange

tug of possessiveness in his heart. The cavemanesque thoughts were piling up, deep and high. *No one talks about my girl like that*. Except, Katlin wasn't his girl. She was just a gorgeous, sassy, fearless woman he had the good fortune of spending time with until she was safe and her memories returned. She'd had a full life already in progress before they'd met. One without him in it. "We don't know anything right now," he said, nonsensically defending her against herself, "other than the fact you're in danger."

Her hand unfurled from its fisted position, and she turned her palm beneath his, spreading her fingers, allowing his to slip between. "The shooter is still out there. What if he never stops coming for me?" she whispered, sounding vulnerable enough to break his heart. "Whoever's behind the gambling is making big money, and I tried to get in the way. No amount of time is going to make someone like that drop the vendetta. And I'm not even the same person I was when I started all this. I can't even remember her."

Jack's heart twisted. "Your memories will return. You need to give it time. And cut yourself some slack. You've got to stop blaming yourself until we have all the facts."

She rolled her head against the seat, looking away from him. "I was nearly killed in the car accident. I lost my memories. I'm shot at daily. Living on the outskirts of nowhere," she said miserably, "practically in witness protection. And I've got no one to blame but me."

Jack released her hand in favor of the wheel and

refocused on the long, dark country road ahead. The sharp edge of her words cut into him, and he cringed with an unexpected lance of pain.

It was clear and reasonable that she'd hate her current situation, but which parts were the worst, and were there any bright spots? Did she only loathe the truly ugly parts, or was he just one more nasty piece in an unwanted box set of awful?

And why did it hurt so much to think that might be it?

"I can't go back to work if I'm on the run," she said abruptly, seeming to catch a second wind. "Even if I get my memories back, I'll have to stay in hiding. If I can't work, how can I live? Afford my rent and bills? I can't even go into actual witness protection because I don't know anything. I've got no leverage."

"We'll figure it out." He cast a glance her way, hating that he hadn't been of more help to her yet, and that despite his best efforts, she was unhappy. "I'll help. Whatever comes, I won't leave you until this is all over and I know you're safe. It's understandable to be scared."

"I'm not scared," she snapped. "I'm angry."

Their eyes met in the dark cab, illuminated briefly by the there-and-gone flash of oncoming headlights.

Jack tensed, then laughed. "Fair." How was he so terrible at guessing her moods? How was she so good at surprising him when so few people ever did?

"I meant it when I said I don't want to be a reporter anymore," she said, "but I also don't want to be a murder victim, so I guess this is my last story.

Which means I have to finish it." She turned to look through the windshield, chewing her lip and working her jaw. "I need to see this through."

"All right, then let's start with a pot of coffee or tea and call Fortress," Jack said, the night's events replaying neatly in his head. "We can trade information and try to work out what it all means. That'll give us a bigger, clearer picture of what we're dealing with. Then we can decide what to do next."

"First, I want to go to the law office," Katlin said. "No one will be there at this hour, and I want to look around without being watched by Marsha, the cleaning crew or a cop. Maybe something there will kick my brain into gear."

Jack frowned, unsure. "I get that you want to be proactive, but I don't think breaking and entering is the way to go right now, especially if you're trying to avoid the police."

"Who's breaking in?" she asked, a sly smile forming on her pretty mouth. "I have a key." She lifted the law-office identification card from her clutch, along with her ring of keys.

Chapter Thirteen

The dark sky opened and rain poured down as Jack parked the truck behind the offices. It had been one hell of a night so far, but he reasoned that the shooter from the docks would be in hiding for a couple of hours while his team of criminals regrouped. "The locks might have been changed," he warned. "If so, we leave."

She nodded. "Got it."

"If anyone's inside, we leave immediately," he continued. "We don't want our names on any more police reports. And you stay where I can reach you quickly in the event things go south."

"Deal." She tugged her door handle, then slipped into the dreary night before he could add another stipulation.

As if he could stop her. He nearly rolled his eyes at the thought.

He followed her to the back door of the law office, vigilant for signs of potential witnesses or shooters.

She dashed through the icy rain expertly and on tiptoes, managing her broken heel like a champ. She swiped her badge, and the small red light flipped to green. The snick of a rolling dead bolt drew a smile on her face.

And an alarm wiped it off.

"Shoot!" Katlin bounded to the keypad beside the door and punched in a code before he could pull her away. The alarm went silent.

They stared at one another in the aftermath, waiting for what would happen next. When nothing did, her shoulders relaxed and the broad smile returned.

"You knew the code," he said, a ribbon of awe and hope winding in him.

"It's the last four digits of my social security number." She shrugged. "They probably make the codes personal so the system can track who comes and goes."

He lifted his eyebrows. "You knew the code," he repeated, and she froze.

Her mouth opened and closed, then she threw herself at him. Her arms circled his waist, and she squeezed him tight. "I know my social security number," she whispered.

His arms curved around her narrow back on instinct. His tall frame curled protectively over her. "Told you," he whispered back. "You've got this."

She wobbled in his arms, and he let her go. "Sorry." She bent to peel off the mismatched pair of heels, one broken and one not. "We should hurry," she said. "Just in case anyone's tracking visitors here. I can see why they might after what happened to Mr.

Fitch." She hurried toward the front of the office and the desk that held all her things.

Jack forced his eyes not to linger on the deeply cut back of her sexy dress or the miles of bare legs visible below a very high hemline. He tried not to imagine running his fingers along that hem, inching it up from behind while planting hot kisses down her bare spine. He didn't mean to wonder what it would feel like to pull her back against his chest and rid her of the little dress altogether...

She turned and caught his eye, a wicked smile stretching over her face. She'd caught him ogling her. Wanting her. And she knew it. "Everything okay?"

"Mmm-hmm." He cleared his throat and nodded into the darkened room. "What now?"

Katlin wet her lips, returning his appreciative gaze and allowing her attention to linger unashamedly in places that made him want to moan. "We think I moved here to chase the gambling story," she said a moment later, slightly breathless. "So I probably got the job here for a reason, too. Maybe for more than just proximity to the college. I could've worked at a fast-food place on campus if that was the only goal. Instead I went after the internship Fitch offered."

Jack nodded. "So what are you thinking?"

"That I was a schemer." She offered a self-deprecating smile. "Cunning, manipulative and possibly not a nice person."

"You were thorough, thoughtful and effective," Jack said. "You had a goal and you went after it.

Griffin would've been very proud. It takes courage to do all the things you did to get to the truth."

She crossed her arms, looking pensive and a little uneasy. "My memories of him feel so close to the surface. Him more than anything else. Something tightens in me every time you say his name, but it's all completely out of reach. I hate it."

"I know." Jack stepped closer, leveling her with his most encouraging stare. "No one can blame you for the frustration, or for anything else you're feeling. You've been through a lot. Are still going through a lot. But Griffin thought you were fearless. He said you faced every trial with your chin up, and he loved that. I think he was right, and I know it helped him worry less about you being here alone in the States."

"It's funny," she said, looking inexplicably guilty and a little ashamed. "Because being afraid is nearly all I've done since I woke up."

Jack pressed his hands to his sides, willing them not to reach for her. To hold and comfort her. Griffin would absolutely not approve of that, and Katlin didn't need more complications in her already messy life. "Well, I think you've handled it all very bravely. Now that we're here, where do you want to look first?"

She released a long, heavy breath. "Right. I'm wasting time." She turned for her desk.

"That wasn't what I meant."

"I think we should look at Fitch's client files. According to the internet, he handled a lot of high-profile white-collar crimes. Mostly mild-mannered schmoes. They embezzled. Committed fraud. Tried to make themselves richer or more powerful. No murderers or career criminals."

"Those white-collar crimes are in-line with what we saw tonight," Jack said. "Fancy dress. Big money. Important people. Could one of his clients be behind the gambling ring?"

Katlin's mouth formed a small O. "That's an excellent theory. Why don't I go through my desk while you take a look in Mr. Fitch's office? We can divide and conquer. Take pictures of whatever you find so we can evaluate it all later, without having removed anything from a crime scene."

Jack smiled. "On it." He moved swiftly into the office where he'd seen officers swarming earlier. The bloodstained carpet was a gruesome indication that this was the right place.

He selected a pencil from the mug on the desk and used it to open and poke through desk drawers.

A small gasp drew his eyes to the doorway a few moments later. Katlin was leaning against the jamb. Pale and unsteady, a visible tremor racked her limbs.

Jack rushed to her side, reaching for her the moment he was close enough. "What is it?"

She accepted his touch, pressing her body against his as she shook. "I don't know. This office just…" Her voice quaked and her teeth began to chatter, cutting off her words. "I have this awful, icy feeling and it's telling me to leave. Now."

Jack rubbed his palms up and down the cool skin of her exposed back. "Here." He released her to slip out of his suit jacket and set it over her shoulders. Something he should've done long before. "We can leave as soon as you're ready."

She nodded, tugging the jacket more tightly around her and pinching it closed at her chest. Beads of sweat clung to her brow despite the visible chills. "I don't know what's wrong with me. I feel sick, dizzy and panicked, but nothing happened. I just walked in here to say my desk was clean. The computer's gone."

Understanding lit in Jack, and he folded her into his arms. He should've recognized the symptoms immediately. He'd seen them countless times. Even experienced them himself. "You might be having a panic or anxiety attack." He caressed her cheek with the back of one hand as he looked into her eyes. "Possibly PTSD. You could've seen something bad in this room. Maybe being here again triggered the reaction."

She sucked in a ragged breath. "What if I was here when Fitch was shot?" she asked, gaze fixed on the bloody carpet stain.

He took her by the hand as he stepped away. "We should go. There was nothing to see here. Fitch's computer is gone, too. Probably taken into evidence by the police."

She backed away from the office, and Jack followed, thankful that they were finally on their way home. *To the safe house*, he mentally corrected, not their *home*. Though a piece of him could see her in his home. In his arms. And in his bed.

"Wait." Katlin drifted into a nook with filing cabinets and storage boxes. She opened one and frowned at the contents. "Who keeps paper files anymore?"

"They could be backups or just old," Jack suggested. "From before everything went digital." He watched as she worked methodically through the drawers and boxes, flicking past names and sliding hanging folders along the narrow silver rails. She stopped at the third drawer of the second cabinet and turned wide eyes on him. "No *P*s." She stepped back to give him a clearer view.

The space inside the drawer, behind a tab with a bolded letter *P*, was empty. There were plenty of files behind the tab with a letter *O*, and lots more crammed into the space meant for files beginning with *Q*s and *R*s, but… "No *P*s," he echoed.

The grin that followed was cut short as a flash of light swept over her face.

Jack ducked into the shadows, pulling Katlin with him.

Beyond the glass back door, a police cruiser was patrolling the alleyway where Jack had parked the truck. An officer climbed out and shined a light into the truck's windows, then circled the vehicle, pausing on the opposite side.

"Did you lock the doors behind you?" Katlin asked.

Jack watched the officer closely as he circled the truck. "Yeah."

"What's he doing?" she asked, setting two small

palms against his chest and drawing Jack's attention to her incredible warmth and nearness.

"I'm not sure." He had to force his thoughts away from the feel of her warm breasts pressed to his torso. When he returned his attention to the alley, the officer was inside his cruiser and pulling away.

"Good. He's leaving, and we should, too," Katlin said.

They stepped carefully out from hiding and made their way toward the back door at the end of the hall.

The jingling and clanking of bells on the opening front door hurried their pace. Katlin swiped her discarded heels from the tile floor, where she'd left them, without missing a beat.

Jack checked in both directions before pulling her outside.

For the second time that night, they hit the pavement running.

He kicked himself mentally for agreeing to bring her here. There was no telling who'd just come into the office through the front door. The police? A shooter? Had Jack put Katlin in harm's way again? Or put her in danger of being arrested for disturbing a crime scene? He had to stop saying yes to her every request like an idiot in… He stopped himself, pulling up short mentally as the final word circled in his mind. *Not like a man in love.* Jack had been in love before, and it hadn't been anything like this. For him and Cara, love had taken years to build. The intense and wholly complicated feelings he'd developed for Katlin were something else entirely. And he didn't have time to think about what they might be.

He beeped the truck doors unlocked as they ran toward the vehicle, now only steps away.

A small red flash beneath the truck slowed his pace, reflecting on a rain puddle near the front wheel. Jack's feet dug into the ground, and his forward momentum ceased with a jolt. Katlin stumbled as their connected arms snapped tight.

"What is that?" she asked, pointing to the crimson shimmer on the water's shallow surface. Her eyes flicked to his in fear and recognition. "Jack?"

A sick sense of realization coiled deep in his gut. His jaw locked and his tongue seemed to swell. He pulled her back, curling an arm around her middle and sweeping her off her feet as he turned for the sidewalk. He managed three or four long, pounding strides before—

Boom!

The truck exploded behind them.

Chapter Fourteen

The world seemed to shake around them. Jack's ears rang, and his vision blurred as he tightened his grip on Katlin and curled himself protectively around her small body. He thanked the stars for their vast difference in size, making it easier to shield her from the flame and debris. They crashed onto the sidewalk in a painful heap, half tripping, half thrown by the force of the blast.

He rolled quickly away from her, careful not to let his heavy and aching body crush hers. Knives of searing pain sliced through his back and shoulder as he pressed against the icy sidewalk, his limbs momentarily weak.

Above him, the night sky quivered with apparitions of heat, and orange flame licked into the air.

"Jack!" Katlin's panicked face appeared in his view. She hovered over him, pressing shaky palms against his beard, jaw and chest. "Jack!"

He pushed onto his elbows with a groan. "Are you okay?" he rasped.

"You're hurt. Bleeding." The terror in her tone

sent a new ache through him. He longed to reassure and comfort her. But they needed to move. If the shooter came by now, they'd both be dead.

"I'm okay," he said, forcing himself into a seated position and squinting to straighten his vision. He needed to get his bearings, then get Katlin out of here. Somewhere safe, where they could call his team and wait for an extraction.

"Your back!" Katlin moved onto her knees for a better look at the damage. "Oh, my gosh. There's so much blood. What can I do?"

He shook his head. "Nothing. I'm fine. Help me up."

"You're definitely not fine." Her small hands pressed against his shoulders, anchoring him firmly to the sidewalk. "You need medical attention. We're staying until you get it."

He wanted to argue, but the fact that he hadn't regained enough strength to shake away her small hands suggested she was right.

The distant cry of sirens slowly carved through his mental haze, and the previous few moments returned to him like a slap. Someone had blown up their ride. Only seconds before they would have been inside.

His focus snapped to Katlin's dirty, scraped-up face. "Are you hurt?"

"No. You're hurt," she said, her voice frantic as she waved her hands helplessly near his shoulder. "Someone blew up your truck. We could've been in it. And your back is burned and bloody." Fear tightened her tone, and emotion colored her cheeks. "There's so much blood. I don't know what to do. How are you not upset? Are you in shock?"

Jack rocked onto one hip with a wince, then freed his cell phone. He pressed his finger against the screen to unlock the device, then passed it to her. "It looks worse than it is. Call Wyatt. Let him know we need a ride."

Katlin took the device and made the call, mumbling under her breath about Jack not being able to see the wounds on his back. How would he know what they looked like? She returned the phone to him with a smug expression. "Wyatt's on the way. He said to make sure you see a medic or he won't let you in his car."

Jack frowned.

The ambulance turned onto the street at the end of the block and rolled slowly in their direction, accompanied by a police-cruiser and fire-truck tail.

Katlin retook her seat at his side, tugging the hem of her little dress as she arranged her filthy, beat-up legs in front of her. "The police are going to know I used my code in the law-office security system," she said. "I'm going to tell them about my amnesia and admit it was a poor decision on my part, but that I'd hoped being somewhere familiar would jar my memories." She leaned against him, and rested her head on his shoulder. "Do you remember how all those *P* files were missing from the drawer?"

He inhaled the unique scent of her, able to identify it even in the midst of chaos, in an alley thick with smoke from the fire. "Yeah." He breathed deeply, allowing the familiar and comforting scent to anchor him. Whatever else had happened, Katlin was okay. He'd protected her. The pride in that realization expanded his chest and refilled his sails.

"I didn't think of it before now," she continued, clearly unaware of the powerful connection and unexpected attachment his heart was revealing. "There was a note on my desk calendar. I was supposed to remind Fitch about a dinner meeting with Peterson on the night of my crash. That's not a coincidence, right?"

Jack pushed to his feet with a groan. "Nope." He needed to get his head in the game.

It was normal to feel attached to someone he'd shared so many near-death experiences with. It was the way he felt about his brothers at Fortress. His brothers from combat. He ignored the voice at the back of his mind that demanded he knew better than that. He'd only felt this way once before, and he knew full well what was happening.

A pair of EMTs launched from the ambulance, now parked at a safe distance from the burning truck.

The fire truck rushed in closer, firemen jumping immediately into action.

Katlin stood and gripped Jack's elbow when he swayed. "You should sit."

"No." He looked her way, his vision focusing and his mind racing. He was eager to leave his unexplored feelings for another time. "Any chance you know that kid Dylan's last name?"

"No, why?"

Jack shook his aching head, sending knives through his brain. "I read an article last night that mentioned the chief of police here. Thomas Peterson. He's got a kid at Centre College."

"Dylan," she whispered.

"Maybe," Jack said, moving slowly to meet the EMTs. "Find out, but don't say more than you have to when the police get here."

"I won't," she agreed, keeping pace easily at his side. "There was a police cruiser out here just before the explosion."

He locked her in his gaze as the EMTs arrived. "I know."

They were in much deeper trouble than he'd imagined.

KATLIN EASED ONTO the couch beside Jack, careful not to jostle him as he rested. His back and shoulders had been singed and cut by bits of flying glass and debris. The paramedics had confirmed what Jack had told her. The wounds looked worse than they were. Lots of blood from multiple fairly shallow lacerations. They'd cleaned and bandaged the worst of it and given him an over-the-counter medicine and a prescription-strength one, then let him go at the scene. Meanwhile, she'd been completely unharmed. A few scrapes and bruises from their awkward landing on the sidewalk, but nothing that needed sutures or a medic's attention. Thanks to Jack.

Her heart warmed as she offered him a cup of

steaming tea. "It's good for easing tension," she said. "You have to relax for optimum healing." A sudden idea of how she might aid him in his relaxation popped into her mind, and she felt her cheeks flush hot with the dirty visual. She'd been learning quickly how many things amnesia hadn't caused her to forget, like the impact physical desire had on a daily routine. Vivid intimate images of her with Jack had interrupted more serious moments and conversations than she would ever admit.

And when Jack had told responding officers that he and Katlin were out enjoying the night together as part of their date when the bomb went off, she'd been shocked at how badly she wished that was true.

Jack hiked an eyebrow. "Katlin?"

"Hmm?" She pressed her lips tight. She'd done it again, wandered into a shamefully lustful daydream while Jack was hurt and miserable. "Sorry, what?"

He shifted for a better look at her, and his broad, muscled arm brushed hers. His skin was warm and flushed from a recent hot shower and the scents of soap and shampoo clung to his clothes, a mere T-shirt and sweatpants. "I said I spoke to my team and researched the chief of police while you were in the kitchen." He handed her the tablet from his lap. "Wyatt and Sawyer are following up on what happened at the docks. Reviewing footage collected from the scene while the place emptied and reaching out to local police contacts for any other information they can get. They're going to call in a few minutes and bring us up to speed."

"Great." Katlin examined the article on the tablet's

screen. A family photo of police chief Peterson, his wife and his son, Dylan, anchored the small write-up. Dylan was younger in the photo and dressed in a private-school uniform, but according to the article, he'd been accepted to Centre College. "So we were right. I'm attending Centre to get to know Dylan and grab the scoop on the gambling ring. I didn't call the police because Dylan's dad is the chief." She looked up. "Do you think that means I didn't want his dad to know I was investigating, or that I thought his dad wouldn't listen if I tried to alert him?"

"I don't know." Jack sipped the tea and grimaced. "This is terrible."

"It's not." Katlin laughed. "It's chamomile."

He nodded in mock understanding. "That's another word for awful?"

"Stop." She shoved his shoulder gently, enjoying the moment of levity before resting against his side. Her gaze landed on the fireplace mantel across from them. Her brother's memorial flag had been placed at the center.

"I hope that's okay," Jack said, following her gaze to the flag. "I saw it with your things and thought it should be displayed."

"Of course." She warmed further to him, even while kicking herself for not having taken the time to put the flag on display. It didn't matter if she remembered Griffin. He'd given his life for her freedom, for their country. He deserved to be remembered, and his memory deserved to be respected. "I look at that flag and something in me tightens," she admitted. A foggy sense of patriotism, or memories for Griffin just out of reach? She couldn't be sure. "I know how important it is and exactly what it means. I wish I could remember him."

"You will." Jack reached for her hand. He curled his strong fingers over hers. "All of this will be over soon, and a year from now it'll probably feel more like a dream than reality, but it will be over."

"Thanks for saying that," she said, her heart expanding impossibly further in appreciation. "I couldn't do any of this without you." She shifted on the cushion for a better look into his sincere hazel eyes. "I'm sorry your truck was blown up. And I hate that you're hurt."

"Thankfully, I'm not nearly as delicate as I look," he said, the corners of his lips curling into a rueful smile.

She rolled her eyes and smiled back. As if anyone looking at Jack Hale could think he was anything less than lethal. The newly shaved head, sexy hipster beard and eight-pack abs screamed dangerous. Add the Green Beret tattoos, and prowling way he moved, and he might as well carry a warning sign. Her favorite part of all was that, for her, he was gentle, sweet and kind. For her, he felt a lot like she imagined coming home would feel.

"And no one cares about the truck," he continued. "There's always another truck. There's only one you. What matters is that you're okay."

There was a new tenderness in his eyes. And it called to her in a way she couldn't ignore.

Katlin set a tentative hand on his chest as their gazes locked. She trailed her fingertips over his soft cotton shirt, enjoying the responsive flex of his pectoral muscles. He watched her closely, expression guarded, as she tested the physical boundaries between them. Katlin wondered if she was right to think he felt the incredible chemistry and unique connection between them, too.

His jaw clenched and his gaze darkened as she inched closer, flattening her palms against the hard planes and ridges of him. She glided her hands tenderly over his ribs and abs, then up and over his shoulders, exploring the nape of his neck before curling her fingers into the fabric of his shirt.

"Thank you for saving me," she whispered. "For protecting me. For coming to the hospital and keeping me alive. Thank you for being kind to me, even when I'm infuriated with myself."

He lowered his heated gaze to her mouth, and her lips parted in response. In request. She longed for him to close the distance and devour her.

A low moan escaped him as he reached for her. He latched steady fingers around her wrists and her heart skittered into a sprint. "Katlin, I can't," he said, and tugged her hands gently away. The expression of utter heartbreak on his handsome face was nearly enough to steal her breath. "I'm sorry."

"Why?" she asked stubbornly, allowing him to drop her hands into her lap. She lifted her chin and ignored the deep humiliation flaring inside her. She longed to run to her room and slam the door, but refused. She knew Jack felt whatever was brewing between them. She'd seen it in his eyes and heard it in his tone.

Hadn't she?

"It's my duty to protect you," he said, his voice gravelly and thick. "I promised Griffin as he died. I made a vow, and I owe him that. So I can't do this." He motioned between them before setting his hands against his thighs. "I'm sorry."

Defiance stiffened Katlin's spine. "That was what Griffin wanted. What do you want, Jack? Not Griffin. You." She waited, hating the conflict in his eyes. "I get that guys want their friends to stay away from their little sisters, but explain to me why. Why wouldn't he want the man he trusted most in this world to be with the woman he most wanted to see most cared for and protected? You're citing guy code as your big reason, but I'm calling your bluff. My brother trusted you with his life. Why wouldn't he trust you with me?"

She relented then, suddenly as disappointed in herself as in Jack. A small, humorless laugh bubbled to the surface, and she shook her head. "You know what? Red-hot chemistry or not, I don't want a man who puts anything ahead of me or ahead of us. So maybe you're right. We shouldn't do this."

Jack's gaze lowered to her mouth once more, and

Katlin cocked an eyebrow in challenge. "What do you say, Jack? Friends?"

A low cuss rumbled in his throat as he reached for her, then wrapped his broad hands around her hips and tugged her close. His eyes searched hers a long moment before he pressed his firm, hot mouth to hers. The taste of chamomile lingered on his lips. His hands moved in tandem up her back, urging her closer. When he tilted his head and swept his tongue across her bottom lip, she yielded eagerly to him, parting and accepting as he deepened the kiss.

Katlin's arms wrapped around his neck, and she stretched one thigh across his lap to straddle him. Her breasts swelled and ached with need and a desperation to be touched by Jack. She imagined him rising and carrying her to his bed. Willed him to touch her more and everywhere as she met his tongue stroke for stroke. She gasped when his hands fell low again, gripping her backside and pulling her hips against him in one powerful move.

Kiss broken, their breaths were short and ragged while they evaluated one another. Her lips tingled from his kiss and every part of her wanted more.

She waited, unsure. She hoped he wouldn't tell her the kiss was a mistake, not when she was certain she had never been kissed like that before. Maybe no woman ever had. The touch, the heat and the connection had been perfection, and now he stared back, speechless.

What did it mean?

Jack leaned his forehead to hers and curled his

solid arms protectively around her back, drawing her to his chest.

In the silence that followed, she could already feel him pulling away.

Chapter Fifteen

Jack fell asleep dreaming of Katlin's kiss. The scent of her skin and taste of her lips. The way her delicious curves fit perfectly against him, and all the ways their bodies could have fit together even better.

And he woke berating himself for the weakness.

Yes, Griffin would want his sister to be happy, safe and cared for, but he would absolutely not want the person meeting all her varied needs to be Jack. He'd made that clear when he'd nearly knocked Jack's head off for commenting on her looks in a photo. If Griffin could somehow know about half the thoughts Jack had had about her since they'd met, he'd be waiting for him on the other side of eternity with a rifle. Or a grenade.

Aside from the guilt of breaking a vow to someone who'd saved his life multiple times and in many ways, Jack wasn't sure how to justify getting physically involved with anyone who was under such duress and without her memories. What if she suddenly recalled she didn't date military men or that she preferred guys with suits and 401(k)s? He cringed internally at the thought. He'd never be a corporate drone. Never willingly push papers and put on thirty pounds while staring mindlessly at a screen full of statistics or client orders. That wasn't any kind of life for him. He grimaced as a far worse thought registered. What if Katlin was one of those women who liked docile, geeky men, not ones who'd survived foreign battlefields when most of their team members hadn't?

He forced himself out of bed with a grunt and headed down the hall for a shower. A cold one.

"Good morning." Katlin's voice rose through the quiet house, drifting to his ears from the kitchen on a whiff of fresh-brewed dark roast. "Coffee?"

"No thanks," he answered, bypassing the bathroom in favor of saying a proper hello to Katlin before getting on with his day. He told himself he was just being polite. He didn't need to see her now that he knew she was awake. It was simply good manners to greet her in person.

"Are you sure?" She stepped into view at the end of the hallway, a steaming mug cradled in her hands. An oversize gray T-shirt hung askew from her narrow shoulders like a nightshirt. Four large black letters stretched across the tempting curves of her chest. *ARMY*.

Griffin's shirt, he realized, feeling the reminder like a kick to his gut.

He lowered his gaze from her apparently braless breasts only to find a perfect set of slender thighs at the hem of the shirt. Bare thighs. And just like that, the fantasies returned. He wanted to greet her

tantalizing mouth with a searing morning kiss, and
satiate her sexy-as-hell body with gratuitous morning sex. And he wanted it more than he wanted his
next breath.

He accepted the mug with a grin, dragging his
gaze back to hers and admiring the heat in her deep
chestnut eyes. "Thanks."

She bit the corner of her lip, honey-blond hair
slightly mussed from sleep.

And he felt the familiar swell of his near-perpetual
erection since meeting her. She knew she got to him,
and damn if he didn't like it.

But he had to keep his head in the game. Before they could be more than just a protector and
his charge, he needed to get her out of harm's way
for good. That meant concentrating on his job. No
more touching. No more kissing. No more moments
of weakness. To do that, he was going to need a much
colder shower than originally planned.

KATLIN CURLED ON the safe-house sofa with her e-reader,
warm beneath a blanket and enjoying a fire in the fireplace. She'd opened a digital book from her library
and was attempting to concentrate on the story line,
but couldn't keep herself from imagining Jack's hard
body in the steamy shower.

She glanced at the clock and frowned. He'd run
off almost an hour ago and hadn't returned. Surely
he was out of hot water by now.

She flipped the pages of her digital book, no longer seeing the words. Her gaze rose to the flag on

the mantel across from her, and realization returned with a snap. Jack was still worried about what Griffin would say, and he wasn't taking an hour-long shower. He was hiding from her.

So much for enticing him with her oversize T-shirt and hot coffee.

She pushed onto her feet and headed down the hallway, hoping she was wrong. With everything else going so poorly in her life, she needed Jack to want her more than he wanted to please her brother. The chemistry between her and Jack had been present since the moment they'd met, and it had grown into something solid and comforting these last few days, not to mention something downright intoxicating. To deny that would be insane and heartbreaking. In fact, with all the awful things they kept facing, it only seemed fair that they should have a little fun. She wasn't trying to rope the man into marriage. It wasn't as if she was falling in love with him. She only wanted to explore what they had going already. Was that so wrong?

The sound of a slamming car door stopped her in her tracks. Her muscles tensed and her senses went on high alert as she imagined the shooter at their doorstep. "Jack," she called, moving quickly down the hall, past the empty bathroom and through the open door to his room.

He closed his laptop and pushed casually onto his feet. He'd dressed in jeans and a Fortress Defense T-shirt that clung to his sturdy frame. "Wyatt's here," he said.

Her shoulders sagged in relief. "Wyatt?"

"Yep." He gave her baggy shirt a cursory glance. "You should probably put on some pants."

Katlin crossed her arms over her chest as Jack slipped past her into the hall, completely unaffected by her yet again.

A moment later, she heard the front door sweep open. "Come on in," Jack said. "Thanks for coming."

The cold sting of rejection slapped her cheeks as she scurried to her room.

Jack had not only been hiding from her, but he'd also called in backup!

She dressed in a rush, sliding into a soft pair of jeans and even softer V-neck sweater. She brushed her hair and dashed her lashes with mascara, her lips with gloss. Whatever the men were talking about, she didn't want to miss it. She hoped the flush of embarrassment was gone as she hurried to meet them, following the sounds of their voices to the kitchen.

"We were able to confirm Dylan is police chief Peterson's son," Wyatt said as she joined them at the table. "Hey, Katlin. How are you holding up?"

"Okay," she said, lancing Jack with a stare. "He was hurt, not me."

Wyatt glanced at Jack, unmoved. "Still, you've had one hell of a week."

"I have," she agreed, not wanting to talk about it. "So we know Dylan is police chief Peterson's son, and that Attorney Fitch had a meeting with one of them on the day he died," Katlin said. Peterson wasn't an uncommon name, but based on everything else they knew, it seemed the sensible jump.

Wyatt nodded. "That's what I'm thinking."

"But we don't know how much the chief knows about the gambling ring or his son's involvement," she said. "Or even if his dinner meeting with Fitch had anything to do with either."

Wyatt rubbed a palm against his stubble-covered cheek. "Right again. I don't suppose you know how we can get our hands on the missing files? Maybe Fitch kept digital backups somewhere."

"Maybe," Katlin said. "I don't remember, but even if there are backup files, we wouldn't be able to access them legally." She tapped her thumb against the tabletop. "Maybe we should take another look inside my apartment. According to Maggie, a friend of mine from the newspaper, I keep the details of my research on a thumb drive Griffin gave me."

"I heard," Wyatt said, looking from her to Jack. "I can go look around for it if you'd like. You'll be safer here. Any idea where you kept it?"

Katlin's head ached, and her jaw set. "No." That was the whole problem, wasn't it? She couldn't remember anything. If she had a clue of what was going on, she probably could have ended it by now. If she'd awoken at the hospital knowing who she was and who had hurt her, she would've made a proper police report and the criminals would be in jail by now. Instead, her inability to recall anything at all meant the person who'd tried to kill her on the highway had gotten several additional opportunities to take a shot. And the gambling ring was still going strong and her boss had been murdered. The frustration built in her like pressure inside a volcano, bubbling and brewing its way to the top. "Excuse me."

She slid her chair away from the table then made her way to the guest room in the safe house. Her temporary home, while she waited for her brain to work properly again.

Tears pricked her eyes, burning and blurring her vision until she reached her bed and fell onto the mattress in exhaustion. This stupid amnesia. This life. Jack's rejection earlier this morning after the most perfect kiss in history last night. It was all too much, and knowing how easily she could fix things with a single memory put her emotionally over the edge.

She wanted to scream and kick and throw things. She wanted to run until her limbs trembled from exertion and her mind cared about oxygen and nothing else.

She wanted Jack to hold her and tell her again that all these bad things were not her fault, and that very soon it was going to be okay.

"Katlin?" His voice pulled her into a sitting position, and she swiped a few renegade tears as they rolled over her cheeks. Why did she have to be so emotional? Why did he always know the exact moment she needed him most? "You okay? May I come in?"

"No."

He narrowed his eyes. "No, you're not okay, or

I can't come in?" He took a tentative step closer, then waited.

She chewed her lip, unable to meet his eyes.

Jack moved to her bedside. "I'd assumed it was all the talk about your awful week that sent you running, but now that I'm here, you look kind of ticked off." He took a seat beside her. "Since you barely know Wyatt, I'll assume I'm the one who made your hit list. I'm sorry."

She pulled her feet onto the mattress and shook her head. "I just needed a minute. Everything feels so overly complicated."

"Want to talk about it?"

"No. I just want my memories back, and I want you to stop avoiding me." She paused to let the accusation settle. In case he hoped she was too dim to have realized what he was doing today. "I can't control either of those things, and letting problems work themselves out isn't what comes naturally to me."

"I'm not avoiding you," he said, sincerity burning in his rich hazel eyes. "Your safety is my number-one priority. My feelings, however? Aren't even in the top one hundred."

"What about my feelings?" she asked, knowing the stubborn protector would likely tell her that feelings had to come second. She hated the rationale and the fact that she understood it even more. What good would it be to act on the frenzied passion that thickened the air between them even now, if the distraction cost them their lives?

"I care about your feelings," Jack answered gently. "That's why I'm here with you instead of out there with Wyatt. I need to know that you're okay. Are you?"

"No." She twisted her lips into a deep frown and held back the need to scream at the unfairness of life.

Jack dipped his chin in acceptance, then opened his arms.

And Katlin fell in. She wrapped herself around him, rested her cheek against his strong chest and let her eyes close, trying to hold the moment inside. His shirt was soft and warm. His arms strong and protective. She longed to be closer, to climb onto his lap and stay there until all the ugly things outside his embrace had long passed.

He rested his chin against the top of her head. "I'm sorry you're going through this."

"Thanks."

"But I'm glad you called me that night," he said.

Katlin pulled in a long uneven breath and tightened her arms around him. "You don't mind being bombed and shot at?"

"I'm getting in loads of cardio."

She laughed and heard his smile in the words.

"Anything for you," he whispered. The words came so softly, part of her wondered if she'd imagined them. Still, her heart ached for the statement to be true. It couldn't be, of course, because there was something he wouldn't do for her. He wouldn't break a promise to her brother.

Thinking of Griffin brought rise to an epiphany of sorts. She wiggled loose to stare at Jack. "I know why my decision to be an investigative reporter feels so unnatural," she said. "I think I did it for him. Not for me." Realizing the incredible pull her brother had on both Jack's life and hers made her wonder if Griffin had been a magician or was just that loved.

Jack's brow furrowed. His eyes darkened. "Who?"

"Griffin," she said, taking Jack's hand. "Now that I can't remember him, I also can't understand why I'd ever have chosen this life. It feels like an act I put on. Pretending to be brave and courageous. I'm none of those things, but I probably wanted to be because it would've made my brother proud, and he'd clearly meant everything to me."

"You never had to try to make him proud," Jack said.

Her heart broke a little more. Because the only person she wanted to be proud of her right now was the man sitting there beside her.

Someone rapped against the open door, and Katlin sprang upright, releasing Jack and moving quickly away.

Wyatt looked at Jack with wicked curiosity, then turned his gaze on Katlin. "He's right, you know? I met Griffin in boot camp, and he adored you. I remember him talking about his little sister more than he talked about some of his girlfriends. He thought you were going to change the world, and he would've done anything for you."

"He'd have done anything for anyone," Jack said, a note of reverence in his tone. "He was one of the best men I've ever known."

"Me, too," Wyatt agreed. He watched Katlin closely, then added, "You'll get your memory back soon, but until then, we'll keep you safe."

She bobbed her head, unable to form words. A thick wedge of appreciation lodged in her throat.

"You like chocolate?" Wyatt asked, unexpectedly changing the subject. "My wife, Violet, baked brownies this morning and sent them over for you. She said people under stress need chocolate."

Katlin felt the tightness in her throat relax slightly and a smile bud on her lips. "I like chocolate."

"Good. Come on." He waved her to join him, then moved out of the room and into the hall.

Katlin followed with Jack on her heels.

"I know no one can replace your brother—" Wyatt said, casting a look over his shoulder "—but you can consider our team your brothers now. Maybe the four of us can fill some small piece of the void left in Griffin's absence."

Jack set a warm hand at the base of her spine, and Katlin felt her shoulders square.

It wasn't fair for her to want Jack to choose between a vow made to a dying brother-in-arms and her. She felt guilty for ever thinking it. She'd never know what it meant or felt like to be in Jack's position, but she knew what it felt like to be her right now, and she stepped away from his touch.

When she gave away her heart, the man had to be all in.

Chapter Sixteen

The sun was high in the sky as Katlin walked with her ridiculously attractive new "brothers," Wyatt and Jack, along the sidewalk outside her house in town. She appreciated the idea of having a team of capable men on her side, and more than one person in her life, but she sincerely hoped Jack didn't think of himself as her brother. That would be definite salt in the wound.

They'd swung by Fortress to collect a new vehicle after they'd finished making a plan for the day, then followed Wyatt to the cottage and gotten to work. They'd searched methodically through every nook and cranny of the older house, nearly taking the adorable home apart board by board in search of the Green Beret–logoed thumb drive where she kept all her research. Yet, they were leaving empty-handed.

They walked with Wyatt to the corner where they'd parked the trucks. They still wanted to give her part-time apartment another look and perform additional reconnaissance however they could. Maybe visit her car at the impound lot during business hours and ask to go through it. Or revisit her cubicle at the newspaper.

Wyatt crossed the street to his truck, then turned back before climbing inside. "Where to next?"

"We'll cover more ground if we split up," Jack said. "We got shot at while visiting the car and at her other apartment. Maybe you can try one of those first. No one will know you." He turned his eyes on Katlin. "We can talk to your friend at the paper again. You'll learn more from her than Wyatt will."

"Sounds good," Wyatt said, climbing into his truck without further discussion. He powered the window down and hung an elbow over the frame. "Touch base when you finish there and we'll choose our next destinations."

Jack beeped the doors unlocked on their new loaner and nodded.

Katlin climbed inside and buckled up, then began a mental list of random questions in search of a memory. Any memory. She'd begun the exercise two nights ago in what was so far a failed attempt to recall her life before the crash.

What's my favorite movie? Favorite color? Song? Scent? Food? Katlin took a silent beat between questions, waiting for an answer to rise from the enormous, endless void in her mind. She curled her fingers in frustration at her sides as she realized she had no idea what her favorite movie or song was, but her favorite color was the unique mix in Jack's eyes. Pale amber and brown irises flecked with bits of baby blue and every shade of green imaginable. Her favorite scent was his cologne. Her favorite food was the soup and toasted cheese sandwiches he'd made her. She moaned at her ridiculousness, then jumped at the sound of her phone.

"Is that you?" Jack asked, pulling away from the curb and heading toward the newspaper.

She wasn't sure if he meant the moan or the phone, but both were true, so she simply said, "Yeah." She answered the call, catching Jack's eye as she spoke. "Hello?"

"Katlin!" Maggie was out of breath on the other end of the line. "Thank goodness. I called you like three times. Where were you?"

Jack glanced back at Katlin as he slowed at the next intersection. His eyebrows rose in question. "Everything okay?"

"I left my phone in the truck," Katlin told Maggie. She'd never dreamed anyone would call. So far, no one had, and everyone she knew or remembered, other than Maggie, was already with her. "Are you all right?"

"I think," Maggie said, the tension leaving her voice by a fraction. "I'm just glad you're okay!"

Katlin glanced at Jack again. "Why wouldn't I be okay?" Tension formed a constricting band around her chest as she waited for the answer. "Maggie?" she persisted, when her friend didn't respond.

"Sorry. I wanted to get a little farther away from the office before saying anything else." Maggie's breaths rasped through the receiver as if she was moving at an exerting pace. "The police are here."

"The police are where?" Katlin echoed, tilting the phone away and pressing the speaker button so Jack could hear her, too.

"At the paper."

"I'm with Jack, and you're on speaker now," Katlin said. "We're headed your way."

"I don't know if that's a good idea," she said. "When I came back from lunch, a bunch of officers were working their way through the room, asking everyone about you. They wanted to know who's seen you and where they can find you. I'm a terrible liar, so I turned tail and left. I don't want to say anything I shouldn't, and even if I manage to say the right words, my face would give me away."

Jack leaned in the phone's direction. "Maggie?"

The truck sped through the next yellow light as Jack's driving grew determined. Something bad was coming, and he felt it, too.

"You need to go back inside," he said. "Someone's surely told them Katlin was in this week and that she spoke with you. Leaving makes you look guilty, and you haven't done anything wrong. We'll come in and talk to the officers."

"I'm not going back," Maggie said, the panic returning to her voice. "They'll ask why I left."

Katlin watched the buildings grow taller in the distance as the downtown skyline came into view. "Where are you now?" she asked. "We'll meet you, then we can go inside together."

"I'm nearly at the corner outside the building. I'll meet you at the café on Main and Frank. You can give me a ride back." The sound of Maggie's heels clicking against the sidewalk grew louder as she increased her pace. "Is this about what happened at the docks last night? Gunfire was reported. That's where you were going. Right? To meet Dylan? Have you done something?"

"No. I haven't done anything wrong. And there was gunfire last night, but no one was hurt, and we left before the shooting began," Katlin said, feeling slightly guilty for the minor fib. She and Jack really had left before the shooting began. But she didn't think this was the time to point out they'd been the cause of those shots.

"Then why are the police looking for you?" Maggie asked. "I know you don't remember me, but you can tell me anything. You know that."

Katlin frowned, unsure she could trust anyone other than Jack and his team. "Why don't you go back inside and tell them we spoke? Tell them the truth. I have amnesia, and I didn't even remember you when I came into the paper."

Whatever the police wanted, it had nothing to do with Maggie, and Katlin hated to think of anyone else being dragged into her mess. "We'll meet you inside. We're only a few minutes away now. I remember that big glass building with the obelisk."

"The bank building?" Maggie asked.

Jack nodded. "Yes. Five minutes. We're catching a light."

"No," Maggie said. "I'll wait. I know where you

were last night and why. I don't want to tell them. That's your information to share."

Jack switched lanes in the intersection and engaged his turn signal.

Maggie swore under her breath. "There's another cruiser up ahead. Looks like he's headed this way," Maggie said. "Change of plans."

JACK PRESSED THE pedal with more purpose and the engine roared. "Stay calm," he instructed. "Find a cluster of people and insert yourself, then tell us where you are."

"I'm going back to the parking garage," Maggie said, voice quivering. "I'll meet you in my car. At least I can lock the doors there. Are you still close?"

"Yes!" Katlin called. "We're at the light two blocks from there."

Jack pressed the mute button on the screen and frowned.

"What?"

"A cop patrolled the street last night before our truck blew up," he said.

Shards of ice sliced down Katlin's spine. "You don't think the uniforms at the office are dirty?"

"Or they could be fakes," he said, racing along the final block to the newspaper.

Katlin's stomach knotted. Neither of those options were good. "Do you trust Detective Reihl?" she asked, recalling the young female detective with her sharp blue eyes and soft, wavy hair. Was she dirty? Or was she an ally?

Jack pulled his cell phone from his cupholder in answer and dialed, pressing speaker as Katlin had done with Maggie's call. "This is Jack Hale," he began.

Katlin removed the mute feature from her phone and spoke absently into the receiver. "We're nearly there." Her attention hung on each of Jack's words to the detective.

Reihl listened quietly as he filled her in on the situation at the paper.

"If you don't feel comfortable speaking to them, you can speak to me," she said.

"Why do I have to speak to anyone?" Katlin asked, jumping in on the conversation. "Why are cops looking for me at my office?"

The pause that followed seemed to stretch on forever as Jack navigated the truck into the parking deck, passing rows of reserved spaces at ground level.

"You're wanted for questioning," Reihl finally explained. "In conjunction with a near-fatal attack on Dylan Peterson, a fellow Centre College student."

"What?" Katlin squealed, angling in her seat to stare at Jack's phone and nearly forgetting her own. "How could I possibly hurt that guy? He's half a foot taller and eighty pounds heavier!"

"Were you at the docks last night?" Reihl asked, her tone smug and self-important.

"You know we were," Katlin snapped. "We were also nearly killed by a bomb an hour later. So when exactly did I have time to beat up Dylan Peterson?"

"You tell me," the detective answered. "Really.

Anytime you're ready. I can meet you at the station. Or how about a cup of coffee? You pick the place."

Katlin wet her lips as Jack set the phone on his thigh and took the spiraling cement ramp to the next level of the underground garage. "What does she drive?" he asked.

"Who?" the detective responded.

Katlin raised her silent phone to her mouth. "Maggie? We're here. What level are you on?"

Jack looked to her phone as he arrived at the next level. "Maggie?"

"What's going on?" Reihl demanded.

"Oh, no," Katlin said, her heart rate climbing. "Maggie!" She yelled into the phone and shook it, as if that would somehow bring her friend's attention back. The call was still going on. It hadn't been dropped or disconnected. So where was Maggie?

"We're looking for a friend of Katlin's," Jack said. "A coworker from the newspaper. She called us, worried, when she saw the police there after lunch."

Katlin searched the rows of empty vehicles for a sign of her friend as Jack drove them slowly around. There weren't any cars with a person in them. There weren't any people at all.

Jack cursed under his breath and slowed next to a red compact car with an open driver-side door.

"Is that her?" Katlin asked.

"No." He shifted into Park and climbed out, pressing a palm in Katlin's direction and leaving his cell phone on his seat. He set one hand on the butt of his sidearm as he approached the car.

Katlin felt the beads of sweat building on her brow.

"Empty," Jack called, jogging back to the SUV. "Reihl." He grabbed the phone off the seat. "Newspaper employee Maggie Franks has been abducted."

"Abducted," Reihl repeated flatly as Katlin's world tilted.

Katlin gripped Jack's arm, attempting to anchor herself before she was swept away in a current of emotion she couldn't come back from. "How do you know? Maybe she went inside the building. Maybe that's not her car."

Jack gave the small red car a remorseful look. "Small red hatchback on level two," he told Reihl, lifting the phone to his lips and shifting his gaze to Katlin. "Driver's door is wide open. No driver. Purse and phone are inside. Newspaper ID badge is on the floorboards."

Katlin clamped her lips tight to stop the vomit from coming.

Maggie was gone, and it was Katlin's fault.

Chapter Seventeen

Jack shifted into Drive and rolled slowly away from Maggie's car. Much as he wanted to stay and keep watch on the scene, instinct told him to get Katlin out of there.

Detective Reihl's voice rose from the cell-phone speaker in blunt, authoritative punches. She would send officers to the parking garage, but she wanted Katlin to meet her immediately. Katlin's expression was weary and skeptical, and she looked more unsure by the minute. More unsure, in fact, than he'd ever seen her, and something in his gut said the meeting with Reihl was a bad idea. Why wouldn't the detective have simply asked Katlin to talk to the officers in the newspaper building or have sent those officers to the garage? Or come to meet her here herself?

Jack circled the block outside the newspaper slowly, counting police cruisers along the south and west corners. Four cruisers in total. Why would it take so many lawmen to ask a few questions?

Katlin raised four fingers toward him and tented her eyebrows as she agreed to meet Detective Reihl at a coffee place near the police station in an hour. Katlin had noticed the number of cruisers, too.

And four was three too many.

Jack made a left at the next light and headed out of town, back to the safe house, where they could regroup.

He disconnected with Reihl. "Someone took Maggie," Katlin whispered, tapping at her own phone screen. "I can't believe it. How is this happening?" She scrolled and searched for something on the device while he kept watch on his rearview mirror.

He couldn't risk being tailed to the only place that had been consistently safe for her. He wanted to gun the engine and reduce the commute time however he could, but being pulled over for speeding or being stopped for any reason seemed like a potential death sentence. At least until they figured out exactly what was going on and how deeply the police were involved.

"Oh, no." Katlin gripped Jack's wrist. "Listen to this. 'Miss Andrews's former employer, local attorney Nathan Fitch, was murdered on the night Andrews went briefly missing—'" Katlin said, attention glued to her phone "'—only to return to the scene of Fitch's murder on the night of an explosion. Andrews has since gone missing again, only hours after the near-fatal beating of Dylan Peterson, a Centre College classmate of hers, and police chief Peterson's son. Local police are now in search of Andrews for questioning. If you've seen her or know of her whereabouts, please contact the station directly.'"

Jack swore and pressed the gas a little harder. "You're being framed."

"For all of it," she said, stunned. "And it doesn't make any sense. Why would I be shooting and bombing and beating people? I was just in a car accident. I only know like five people!"

"People believe what they read," he said. "They don't care if it makes sense." If the article was right, and the police were really looking for Katlin, even the safe house wouldn't be safe for long. "Maybe we should talk with the doctor from the hospital," he suggested. "She can explain about your memory loss. That might help build your case."

"My case?" Katlin turned wide eyes on him. "You think I might really be arrested for all this?"

"Right now, I think anything's possible, and you need to be prepared. We should probably also contact an attorney and get your story on record."

Katlin straightened, her gaze darting around the world outside the truck. "Where are we going? We need to find Maggie."

"To the safe house," Jack answered, bristling at her angry expression. "I need to figure out how best to protect you while we get answers."

"Who cares if I get thrown in jail? Maggie is in serious and imminent danger. We have to look for her! Reihl barely acknowledged that she'd been abducted. All she cared about was meeting with me, and you're leaving town?"

Jack worked to remain calm. Katlin was clearly upset about her friend in danger, but he doubted that fear held a candle to the gut-wrenching, heart-slicing agony he was hoping not to show. Katlin was in danger, and he needed to protect her. To save her. He needed *her*. He swallowed hard and hoped his voice wouldn't betray him. "We'll find her," he promised, "but first we need to figure out where to look. And being arrested isn't going to help Maggie, so please don't say that again. Besides, if there are guilty cops looking for you, the last place you want to be is in their house."

Her skin paled in understanding. "Right. Okay. So, what first?"

He clenched his jaw, working through the tangle of emotions and possibilities. "I think speaking to your doctor at the hospital will help. She documented your situation, diagnosis and medical status. Those records could be important if things get any worse for you." He glanced in her direction when she didn't respond.

She'd turned her face away, scanning the scenery as it passed. "Maybe."

"Maybe?" His heart sank and his temper flared as a new realization hit. "You didn't tell her about your memory loss."

Of course she hadn't. The Katlin he'd met in that hospital room had been scared and anxious, desperate to get out. Telling the truth meant potentially being asked to stay, and she'd made it clear to him immediately, staying wasn't an option.

"I couldn't," she said. "I had to get out of there. I didn't know you then, but I had to trust you when I knew something was wrong. That someone wanted to hurt me. I'm sorry I lied." She turned repentant eyes on him. "I was scared and confused and I knew I'd die if I stayed."

Jack rubbed a heavy palm over his bearded cheeks and chin, then turned back to the road.

They made the rest of the trip to the safe house in silence.

Inside he spoke to Wyatt by phone about the missing woman, the police and Reihl while Katlin paced a small circle around the living room. He understood why she'd lied to the hospital staff, but he hated that she'd lied to him. And she'd continued allowing him to believe the lie, even after all they'd been through. How had she never found a moment to tell him? What if her head injury had been worse than they'd imagined, and no one knew because she'd kept such an important detail from the medical staff? And he'd whisked her away from the care she'd needed... What if something terrible had gone wrong while they were alone together, and he'd had no idea how to help her?

His heart and mind rejected the possibility of losing her. He'd loved and lost once and swore he'd never put himself through that again. The thought pulled him up short. Was that what this was? Love? No. He shook away the crazy thought. It was the complication of too many emotions tied to one human. Too many years of hearing her praises through the closest friend he'd ever had, then meeting her in person only to find himself powerfully physically attracted to her. To top that off, the time he'd spent with her had proven her to be all her brother had claimed and more. Katlin was strong and determined. Resourceful and smart. She was valiant, and he was honored to be useful to her at all. And if he allowed himself to think of the kiss they shared…

He couldn't do that. He also couldn't help wondering if he and Katlin would've hit it off at all if they'd met under other circumstances. He wasn't quite sure why she would possibly need or want him when she had complete control of her faculties. Because even without her memories, Katlin was a force to be reckoned with, and he was struggling to keep up.

He disconnected with Wyatt, then set his hands on his hips. "The team's looking into Maggie's disappearance. They'll reach out to her close friends and family and make certain a proper missing-persons report is filed." Just in case there was a reason that local PD didn't do that. "Sawyer's already on his way to the newspaper to take down cruiser numbers and find out if they're real or imposters. I sent Wyatt to meet Detective Reihl at the coffee shop. For what it's worth, I have a feeling she's one of the good guys, and I think Wyatt might be able to get her to see what we see. If the police force is contaminated, we need at least one ally on the inside."

Katlin stopped to stare at him, her face red with barely tamped emotion. "Someone nearly killed Dylan last night. Would the chief of police really hurt his own son?" she asked. "If Peterson is part of the gambling ring, then I can understand his determination to get rid of me. Breaking the story would ruin his side business and his career. He'd be humiliated and jailed. But why would he hurt his own son?"

Jack had considered those same thoughts and questions while driving back from town, but he didn't have any answers. "The chief can be involved without being in control." At least that was his best guess. "Maybe he was bought off or threatened. We just don't know."

"Yeah, well, abducted people rarely make it home, and they're usually dead within seventy-two hours. So we need to figure this out fast because Maggie's life depends on it."

KATLIN DRAGGED OUT her laptop and got comfortable at the small kitchen table. She pulled up the local news sites and scanned the articles in search of other shootings, bombings or gambling busts. Something else both violent and uncommon in the days, weeks or months before her car accident. What had gotten her started down this awful path? What had first made her suspect there was an illegal gambling ring at Centre College?

She stopped on an article from nearly a year ago. The reporter, A. Young, had declared an uptick in local busts and arrests consistent with what movies and television often referred to as evidence of organized crime. The article went on to warn readers that while authorities readily dismissed the reality of a modern-day Mafia, especially in central and northern Kentucky, the signs were all there. Furthermore, the reporter had shared the name and photo of one man frequently questioned and released by area police in conjunction with these crimes. Donald Rosch.

Her heart rate soared as she considered the possibilities. Was this the idea that had gotten her started? Could this reporter have more information on what she'd been up to? A few frenzied searches for the name Donald Rosch revealed a multitude of arrests and dropped charges, as A. Young had claimed. Money laundering, extortion and gambling, to name a few. Next, she searched for the brave reporter. She had a growing suspicion that if she could talk to A. Young, she'd discover it wasn't the first time they'd spoken.

She opened a new tab on her laptop, leaving her other searches up to show Jack when he came to check on her. Then she typed *A. Young name* into the search engine beside the name of the small newspaper that had published the article on organized crime.

"How's it going?" Jack called, arriving in the kitchen as she hit Search.

He stripped off his barn coat and toed out of his boots near the door. "It's getting cold out there." He rubbed his big palms together and puffed breath against them. "I added cameras to the mailbox at the road so I can monitor traffic in either direction, and set sensors about ten feet in to alert us if anyone is bold enough to use the driveway."

"Good. No surprises," she said.

He winked. "You got it. Tell me there's coffee."

"I made a pot." Katlin smiled, thankful to have Jack close once more. "We should order dinner in," she suggested. "You've been making every meal, and I've just found a thread I want to pull."

He poured a cup of coffee and set the steaming mug beside her on the tabletop. "Delivery sounds great. I can't eat anything else from a can or the freezer." His brow furrowed. "What kind of thread?" he asked, taking a seat in front of the mug.

"Here." She angled her laptop to give them both a good view, then clicked the first link in her search results and turned back to him. "A reporter wrote an article last year claiming an emergence of organized crime in the area, and I have a feeling it's what got me started. I want to see what you think."

"Katlin." Fear marred Jack's handsome face as his gaze trailed over the screen.

She turned for a look at the article and felt her stomach drop.

Rising Junior Reporter Dead in Single-Car High-Speed Crash

Chapter Eighteen

Katlin placed an order for two authentic Greek gyros, spanakopita to share and a double order of *loukoumades* from a restaurant named Acropolis. She'd found the menu, along with multiple others, in a folder on her laptop titled Heaven. She hadn't been sure what she'd thought she'd find inside when she'd first double-clicked the small manila icon, but a collection of downloaded carry-out menus hadn't been it. Still, she and Jack were both hungry, and they had a lot to think about.

She placed the order through the website after asking Jack what he liked, then guessing for herself. The food would be delivered in thirty minutes, and neither she nor Jack would have to risk venturing out again today. Also a solid win.

Jack finished another call and tossed his cell phone onto the table with a sigh. He ran his fingers over his freshly shaved head and raised warm hazel eyes to her. "Any trouble placing the order?"

"No. Any trouble with the reconnaissance?" she

asked, trying not to admire the shape of his mouth or recall what it had felt like on hers.

He locked his fingers behind his head, showing off a set of impressive biceps. "Wyatt said Reihl wasn't thrilled to see him show up instead of you, but she heard him out, and she didn't push him to disclose your location right now. A good sign I was right to think we can trust her."

Katlin released a long, slow exhale, feeling the tension in her shoulders subside. "Good."

Reihl hadn't exactly given a warm or encouraging vibe when they'd met before, but maybe that was understandable. From an outsider's perspective, Katlin supposed she looked pretty shady, or at least of a questionable character. How else would anyone become involved in such a mess? Regardless, it was good to have someone in law enforcement on her side. "What about the police cruisers outside the newspaper? Real or imposters?"

He dropped his arms to his sides and collected his phone. "We don't know. They were gone when Sawyer got there."

Katlin rolled her neck as the tension returned. "What did Reihl say? Was she angry? Did she think he was just covering for me?"

Jack smirked. "I don't know, but you can ask him yourself. He's hungry and loves Acropolis, so he's on his way over."

Katlin smiled. "Perfect. I never know what's going to happen next around here, so I ordered plenty of extra food. I figured we could heat it up tonight or tomorrow as needed."

"Smart." He watched her, his gaze darkening as it dropped to her lips.

Katlin smiled, enjoying the flash of desire on his handsome face.

That damn undeniable connection, she thought. It was obvious that he had guilt over kissing her. A misplaced desire to be true to her brother. And he probably felt like he was taking advantage of her and the situation since she'd had a number of recent traumas and a head injury, but she doubted anything could change the chemistry sizzling between them. In fact, she had a feeling the bond that had blossomed between them at first sight, then bloomed at a break-neck pace, would've happened regardless of when they met, whatever the circumstances.

Jack's gaze snapped quickly back to her eyes. "We should probably turn on the news," he said, pushing back to his feet. "See if there's any mention of Maggie's disappearance and what local reporters made of all those officers at the paper."

Katlin set aside her laptop, then followed him to the couch. She could only hope there was more information available on the news than she'd been able to find online, which was nothing.

Jack powered on the television, then pumped up the volume when a man appeared behind a podium with the local police department's insignia. A banner along the screen's base declared: Thomas Peterson, Chief of Police.

Katlin perched on the cushion's edge, wishing she could read lips as the man on-screen began to speak. Dramatic breaking-news music played over his words, and a reporter's voice announced, "A press conference held earlier today revealed that an undercover team was assigned to Centre College after allegations of an illegal gambling operation were reported."

Katlin kneaded her hands, desperate to know what the outcome had been, and praying the chief hadn't named her as the criminal mastermind.

"Those allegations were thankfully proven to be nothing more than a hoax."

"A hoax!" Katlin squeaked. "Are they kidding me?" She looked to Jack. Surely this was a joke.

The regretful set of Jack's jaw said it all. He watched the screen carefully, evaluating, she supposed, and was likely seeing more than she could as frustration welled in her soul.

The reporter's voice was replaced by Chief Peterson's as the press-conference clip played on. "My love for Centre College goes back to my days as an athlete and student there, and it carries on through my son, Dylan, today. His dedication to the school, staff and student body is unparalleled. In fact, our entire family has an incredible sense of Centre pride, as do many of you, I know. I can only hope that you will all remain vigilant in your care and concern for our community. I would much rather have spent the time and resources to have my team determine the allegations a hoax than to have allowed something illegal to carry on in our beautiful town."

Jack leaned forward, resting his elbows on his knees. "He's sweating."

"What?" Katlin squinted, trying hard to focus while she mentally reeled over the public announcement. The gambling ring she'd been investigating, the one that had held an event she'd attended, had supposedly never existed. The camera angle changed, and a drop of sweat glistened on Peterson's temple. More gathered near his brow. "You're right."

"He's uncomfortable," Jack said. "He's saying the right words, using the right tone, but he's fidgeting with the notes on the podium and looking away from everything. The people and the cameras."

Katlin shot Jack a look. "Because he's lying?"

"Maybe." Jack didn't look so sure. "His body language seems to say he's under duress. Maybe because he's lying publicly like this. There won't be any room for denial if he's caught. Or maybe he doesn't want to be there at all."

"The press conference wasn't his idea," Katlin said.

The press-conference clip ended, and the station cut to a commercial.

Jack muted the television and turned to her. "I don't think he had his son beaten up, or even allowed it. I think Dylan's beating might've been a warning from whoever's in charge."

"Rosch?" she asked.

"Maybe." The alarm on Jack's phone went off, and he pulled the device in front of him. "Someone tripped the sensors."

"Wyatt or gyros?" Katlin asked, hoping it was one or the other and not an ambush. She wasn't sure she could take that. Not here, in the only place she'd felt safe since waking in the hospital.

"Gyros." Jack handed her the phone and went to answer the door.

Katlin watched the screen, tracking a compact car with Acropolis logos on its hood, door and roof as it rolled slowly down the long lane. When the vehicle stopped near the porch, a man got out, secured his uniform ball cap, then pulled a number of white-logoed bags into his arms. The insignias on his button-down shirt and hat matched the advertisements on the car.

She met Jack at the door so she could take the food while he paid the driver.

At the door, Jack gave the man a long once-over before dropping his hand away from the gun in its holster at his back.

Minutes later, the delivery guy was long gone and Katlin had set the table for three.

Her stomach growled as the delicious scents of seasoned lamb, olive oil and thyme lifted into the air. The onions, feta and orzo called to her as she stared longingly at the steaming containers. "We should probably wait for Wyatt, right?" She bit her lip, hoping she was wrong.

"Nope." Jack handed her a plate and napkin. "Food's hot and we're hungry. He can reheat it if it cools before he gets here."

A smile split her face as she dug in.

They ate in companionable silence for several minutes, Katlin at an embarrassing speed, and Jack in a calmer manner. She hadn't realized just how famished she'd been until the first bite had hit her tongue. The folder from her laptop hadn't been a joke. The gyro really was heaven.

Her eyelids dipped, and she caught herself as her head tipped forward, as well.

"You okay?" Jack asked, the word slightly muffled from his mouthful of food.

She nodded, taking a quick internal inventory to be sure that was true. She was tired. That was to be expected given her level of continuous stress and lack of sleep this week. But it was more than that… She felt oddly, suddenly, fatigued. Her hands and face were slightly numb, like the warm buzz from a second glass of wine. Except, she hadn't had any wine. Her gaze dropped to the delicious meal before them. "Jack…" Her thoughts evaporated as the room dimmed and the floor rushed up to meet her.

JACK SHOT TO his feet as Katlin collapsed. "Katlin!"

He pressed a palm to the table to steady himself when the world tilted slightly. The room shimmered as he lowered slowly onto the floor beside her. "Katli—" His tongue thickened and the word slurred. What was happening?

The floor spun as he reached for the cell phone he'd left on the table. The screen blurred before him as he pressed his fingertip to the unlock button. Beside him, Katlin was motionless and silent. A tidal wave of fear crashed over him. Was she dead? Had they been drugged? What had he missed? And how? His finger thumbed awkwardly across the number 9 on his dial pad. He blinked in concentration as he searched for the number 1. His eyelids drooped farther, felt heavier, and the world around him became a smear of colors.

Boom!

He started at the sound, unable to rise from the floor. Ears ringing, he rolled onto his back and watched as a set of legs strode into view, the front door swinging open behind them.

The delivery man crouched and smirked. "Enjoy your meal, Mr. Hale?"

Jack opened his mouth to cuss, spit and threaten. *Get away from her or I'll kill you. I love her, and I won't let you take her. My team is on the way. I have you on camera. You won't get away with this.* Rage built in his core, words piling on his useless tongue. The phone clattered to the floor, released by his numbing fingers. And the gun at his back was pressed securely against the floor beneath him.

The man scooped Katlin into his arms then tossed her headfirst over one shoulder. "I'll just take this and be on my way. I noticed the sensors in the drive.

Nice touch—too bad they didn't matter." He tipped his hat and strode away.

Jack was left alone with his muddled thoughts, overwhelming fatigue and the sense of having watched his heart be torn from his chest.

He'd done everything right, and he'd failed her.

Chapter Nineteen

Jack's head pounded. A cacophony of sounds pierced his aching temples, and his gritty eyelids fought against him as he forced his eyes open. A groan spilled out as he worked himself up onto his elbows and forearms.

"Whoa!" a familiar voice boomed, distinguishable among the myriad of others. A heavy hand pressed against his shoulder, flattening him to the mattress. "Take it easy, cowboy." Wyatt's gentle drawl removed a bit of Jack's edge, but none of his confusion.

Distant beeping, ringing and footfalls echoed in his head. The squeak of shoes against a polished floor. The rattle of what? Metal carts? Wheels?

He tried again to get his squinting eyes open, despite the barrage of obnoxious fluorescent lighting. The effort paid off at a cost. Searing pain cut through his retinas, blasting straight to his brain. Sudden intrusive scents of bleach, stale coffee and bandages assailed his nose as his senses returned in full force. His stomach lurched in response.

He gripped the bed's edge and fixed one eye on

Wyatt, allowing the other lid to droop. "Where's Katlin?" he groaned, his first words coming low and gravelly. "Is she okay?"

"Take it easy," Wyatt said, crossing his arms and scowling, a look Jack recognized as concern. "Get your bearings first. Then we'll work through the details."

Jack pulled his lips back in a feral show of teeth, unable to control the hostility brewing in him. "Talk."

Wyatt narrowed his eyes, but nodded. "The doc says you're going to be fine. The drugs you ingested were intended to immobilize, not kill. I'm just damn grateful I was held up in traffic downtown or we'd all have been knocked out. That'd be a real mess right now."

"What drugs?" Jack asked, the words raking from his dry, scratchy throat. He searched his mind for answers and waited for the memories to come. "The delivery food," he rasped.

Wyatt nodded.

Fear leached into Jack's skin like icy water through cloth. "Katlin," he murmured, sweeping his gaze around the stark white room. If he'd ingested enough drugs to lay him up like this, what had those same drugs done to her small and delicate frame? "Where is she?"

"We don't know."

Jack's gaze snapped back to Wyatt, his lips curling in rage once more. "Explain. Quickly." He winced against the noise of a busy emergency room. The hustle of staff and worried loved ones. The distant cry of a child.

"You ordered delivery," Wyatt began. "From Acropolis. Your delivery driver was knocked out and carjacked after leaving the restaurant. His attacker put on the uniform shirt, drugged the food then followed the GPS to your place. Stop me when it sounds familiar."

Jack cursed.

"Right," Wyatt continued. "The safe-house door was open when I arrived. You were on the floor. Katlin was gone. I called 911, and here we are. Sawyer's with the police at the farmhouse looking for leads. Cade's speaking with the driver and restaurant staff in town, hoping to get a bead on how this happened, but we think we have a good idea."

Jack levered himself upright once more, this time feeling less like a bag of sand and more like a soldier with a mission. He pulled the IV from his arm and thanked the powers that be no one had taken his clothes and dressed him in a cape that closed in back. "We've got to go."

Wyatt swung his arms apart like an umpire and widened his stance. "No, you don't. You need to rest while the drug runs its course, and you need those fluids to expedite the process." He pointed to the discarded IV. "You're not being admitted, but you're also in no shape to walk out."

"Get out of my way." Jack scanned the curtained-off area for signs of his coat and boots.

"Hey. We need you at full mast," Wyatt said, his

voice smooth and placating. "Just lie down. Heal up and let us work. We've got this, brother."

Jack planted sock-covered feet on the floor. "Where are my boots?"

Wyatt crossed his arms, defiant for a moment, then wised up. "The nurse is going to have a fit when she comes to check on you and sees you're gone."

Jack shared a few expletives, and was handed his boots. "Thank you. Now help me up. I'll recover as we go."

Wyatt shook his head, curved an arm around Jack's back and helped him onto his feet. They moved steadily through the busy emergency room, avoiding eye contact and never slowing down as they exited the treatment area and cut across the waiting room toward the massive sliding glass doors.

A few people stared, but no one tried to stop them. Smart. Because Jack was in no mood for nonsense.

A blast of icy wind beat against him as they exited the building, pulling yet another cuss from his lips.

"Sorry, I didn't think to grab your coat when they loaded you into the ambulance," Wyatt said.

Jack grunted, concentrating to keep his feet in motion.

Inside Wyatt's truck, Sawyer's voice boomed across the speakers, calling to check in before they'd made it out of the lot. "I've got something here at the safe house," he said as they barreled away from the hospital, into the painfully bright, cold day.

"You know who did this?" Jack asked, wincing at

the snarl in his voice and pain that followed through his head.

"No, but I know how," Sawyer answered. "Cade said the folks at Acropolis told him you placed the order online. You didn't call or stop in. Your phone wasn't tapped, and you weren't being followed."

Jack circled a finger in front of the dashboard, wishing Sawyer would hurry up and get to the parts he didn't already know. "Yeah, and…"

"Cade called me, and I spoke with a crime-scene guy collecting evidence here at the farmhouse. He looked at her laptop, and guess what he found?"

"A bug." Jack's addled mind quickened as adrenaline burned through his veins. "Of course." They'd recovered the laptop from her cottage home in town, thinking it was a treasure, though nothing on it had been especially useful. "We brought it from her place. It's open all the time. She's been researching and trying to find answers."

"Yeah, well, someone's been watching and listening," Sawyer said.

Jack gritted his teeth. For all his efforts to keep her safe, he'd willingly carried a Trojan horse into their safe house. And someone with the know-how had infiltrated the device, accessing its microphone and camera features. "They heard us choose a restaurant," he said, putting the details of his tragedy du jour together.

"We think so," Sawyer said. "Then all they had to do was go down to Acropolis and wait for the order to leave the building."

Wyatt kept a steady watch on the rearview mirror as he switched lanes and made several unnecessary turns to be sure no one followed, a practice Jack also employed. "Why do you think they didn't kill these guys?" he asked, shooting an apologetic look in Jack's direction. "I mean, I'm glad they didn't, but they had a chance to finally shut Katlin up and didn't take it. Why?"

"Maybe they still need her for something," Sawyer answered across the line. "Any ideas what that could be, Jack?"

He scrambled for a clue, but didn't have one. "If they've been listening, they must know she doesn't have her memory by now. She's useless for information. If she wasn't, we'd already be building a case against whoever this is." Possibly Donald Rosch, he thought, recalling one of their last conversations. A possible local crime boss.

Wyatt hooked another right and headed for the highway, back to home base, Jack realized—Fortress Defense. "What's important," Wyatt said, "is that they still need something from her. That means they'll keep her alive until she can give it to them. And that gives us time to find her."

Jack curled one hand into a fist on his lap. "We've been looking for a thumb drive her brother gave her. Her friend Maggie said Katlin kept all her research on it. I'll bet they're looking for that, too. They probably heard us talking about it." Once Rosch realized she had evidence against him, it wouldn't be enough to simply shoot her. First, he'd need to destroy whatever dirt she'd collected.

"Maggie?" Wyatt asked. "From the newspaper?" His expression tightened, saying what he wouldn't. *The other woman who'd been abducted today.*

"That's her." Jack worked to steady his breaths and push past the pain ricocheting through his head to his heart and back. "If we find the drive and we get someone at the local PD to leave the computer compromised and available to us, maybe we can use it to communicate with whoever's been listening. We can offer a trade. The information they want in exchange for the women."

Wyatt returned his attention to the road. "All right, men. Sounds like we've got a plan."

"Roger," Sawyer agreed. "I'll catch Reihl and pull her aside. See if she can help."

Jack froze. "Reihl's there?"

"Yeah," Sawyer answered. "I think she's okay, man. We can trust her."

Wyatt nodded, and he hoped they were right. Because Reihl was suddenly their only hope.

Jack had to find Katlin and protect her the way he promised Griffin he would. Then he needed to tell her the thing he'd been stupidly, stubbornly, holding back.

He was deeply and completely in love with her.

KATLIN WOKE ON the ground, consumed by cold and darkness. Damp scents of earth and decay tainted the air. Her mind struggled to make sense of her circumstances. Where was she? And why?

She rolled toward a distant shaft of light, high in the air, squinting and willing her stinging eyes to focus. The hard, gritty ground scratched at her arms and fingers as she struggled to orient herself in the space.

"Katlin?" Her name lifted in the darkness, so quietly she wasn't sure it was real. "Katlin?" The word came again, louder the second time and accompanied with short scurrying sounds.

She turned in search of her company, daring to dream that she wasn't alone, and that there might still be hope in this strange and terrifying scenario.

"You're awake." Maggie's tear-streaked face came into view, disrupting the stream of dust motes in the single shaft of light.

Maggie's hair was tangled and littered with debris, hunks of dirt and splinters of wood. Her eyes and cheeks were red and puffy, as if she'd been extremely ill or crying a long while. Her shirt, filthy and torn at the collar, was in worse shape than her hair. Desperation tightened the corners of her mouth and there were deep lines across her forehead.

"Where are we?" Katlin asked, forcing her body into a sitting position then cringing at the bullet-hot pain that exploded in her head. She pressed a tentative hand to her temple, then patted gingerly along her scalp in search of blood or injury.

"You were drugged," Maggie said, taking a seat beside her and pulling thin legs to her chest. She wrapped her arms around them and rested her chin on her knees. "I heard them joking after they left you here, and I saw the delivery uniform your guy was wearing. Acropolis," she added sadly. "You always liked that place. I thought you were dead."

"Back at ya," Katlin said, working on a smile. "Someone took you from the garage."

She nodded. "My guy knocked me out when I fought him. I didn't recognize him, and I haven't seen him since he left me here. Someone opens the door now and then to toss bottled water down the steps. Sometimes they add a box of crackers or dry cereal, but they never cross the threshold. I don't know if that's good or bad."

"How long have I been here?" Katlin asked, struggling to clear her thick, achy throat.

"They brought you in yesterday. I had to check to be sure you were breathing. You were so still. I sat with you through the night. I was trying to reach the window when you woke. You were shivering earlier, but there's nothing to cover up with."

At the mention of temperature, Katlin felt the chill return. She wrapped an arm around Maggie's back and rested her head on her friend's shoulder. "Thank you." She imagined Maggie attempting to reach the narrow window high above and realized they were in a basement. "I'm so sorry I dragged you into this." And Jack, she thought. She and Jack had been drugged. She and Maggie abducted. All of it was her fault.

Maggie snuggled close and patted her hand. "It's

what we do, right?" she asked. "Reporters have to know the truth. Have to scoop the story." She sighed. "If we live, I'm getting a job at a wedding magazine instead."

"Fair," Katlin said, choking back a half laugh, half sob. "We're going to get out of here. Together. Any idea where we are?"

"Kind of," Maggie said. "We're on the west side. Not far from where you crashed, I think. I saw the exit sign when I was being brought here. After that, I'm not sure. I was in and out of consciousness." She angled her head to reveal a large purple knot on the back. "Pistol-whipped. Not too many girls our age can say that. Maybe I'll put it on my résumé for the bridal magazine. What do you think?"

"Good idea." Katlin wanted to laugh at her friend's joke, but something about the room was eerily familiar. She stared at every brick and corner, letting the basement's menacing vibe curl deep into her aching head and twine with her thoughts. Slowly, an icy finger scraped at the place where her memories had been locked up for too long.

She twisted onto her hands and knees, then stretched slowly to her feet, ignoring the weakness in her limbs and the sway of her stance. She turned in a slow circle, taking in the dark, dank space and willing the icy finger in her head to slice through the fog.

"Donald Rosch," she said, the name rolling off her tongue before she'd made the mental decision to say it aloud. "Donald Rosch is a crime boss who has the chief of police under his thumb. He's using Dylan as leverage to force Chief Peterson into looking the other way while he carries on with business as usual. Rosch has pop-up gambling events all around town, specifically targeting coeds and highly funded private schools like Centre College."

She slapped a hand across her mouth to stifle the building cheer. "Maggie," she whispered against her frozen, filthy skin. "I remember everything!"

Chapter Twenty

Jack prowled through the safe house, scrutinizing every inch of the property, inside and out, while his team met with Detective Reihl for their marching orders. Fortress Defense had officially partnered with the young detective to find Katlin and Maggie as soon as possible. The collaboration should have made Jack feel better, but it didn't. He doubted anything would until he saw Katlin home safe.

He lowered to his hands and knees for the tenth time, running his fingertips over the floor where he and Katlin had fallen after ingesting their drugged meal. Whoever had taken her had left no trace. No sole marks from his shoes, no dropped receipts, ticket stubs or other pieces of investigative gold that always seemed to turn up on television and in movies.

His eyelids drifted shut, willing the memories to return. Instantly, he recalled the scents of the meal, heady and strong. Olive oil, seasoned lamb and feta. His head buzzed lightly in remembrance. He'd assumed the cause was fatigue or stress. Then she'd mumbled his name, gone limp and fallen. He'd dove for her, clumsily, limbs heavy as he landed in a heap at her side. He recalled the explosive sound of the front door being broken in and the steady footfalls that came for her. The delivery man had returned. The delivery man had been a criminal, and Jack hadn't had a clue until it was too late.

He rocked back onto his feet and scrubbed angry hands over his face and head. Hopefully his teammates were having better luck turning up something useful.

Wyatt, Sawyer and Cade had split up to check out Katlin's apartments, offices and car. Meanwhile, Reihl was reviewing surveillance footage from the newspaper, parking garage and Acropolis, looking for a clue as to who had abducted Katlin and Maggie. Reihl had already confirmed the four cruisers Jack had seen outside the newspaper were fakes. It was the reason she hadn't sent the officers to the parking garage immediately after discovering Maggie's abduction. They weren't her men, and she'd known with certainty then that Jack and Katlin's accusations were true. The information was as encouraging as it was disconcerting to Jack. There weren't eight bad cops, but there were eight criminals convincing and well-funded enough to fool everyone.

His phone rang as he made another loop around the space, glaring at the place where he and Katlin had separated. "Hale," he answered, heart rate rising in anticipation of a solid lead and dreading the possibility of more bad news. It'd been more than twenty-four hours since he'd awoken in the hos-

pital and initiated an all-out hunt for Katlin, his...
The thought brought him up short. His what? Katlin
wasn't *his* anything. And that was his fault. She'd
been clear about her intentions. She wanted him and
wanted him to want her. He'd been the stubborn one.
The stupid one. Not seeing the truth for what it was.
Griffin hadn't wanted Jack to lust after his sister,
but Katlin was right—Griffin would never tell him
not to love and cherish her. And the way his every
fiber ached at the thought of losing her, he knew loving and cherishing her was exactly what he wanted
to do. Every day of her life, if she'd let him. And he
should have told her all that sooner.

"I'm on," Sawyer said, responding to Jack's greet-
ing.

"Yep," Wyatt answered. "Cade?"

"With ya," Cade confirmed.

"All right," Wyatt said, taking the reins, as always. "Gang's all here. How are you holding up,
Jack?" he asked.

Jack groaned. "That's going to depend on what
you've got for me."

The long beat of silence that followed was a deaf-
ening answer to his question.

"Hang in there," Wyatt encouraged. "We've all
been where you are. We get it. And we're going to
help you get through it."

Over the course of the past year, each of Jack's
teammates had fallen in love. Each man with a
woman he'd been dispatched to protect, and they'd all
nearly lost her at some point. Jack had been around

for the terror and the aftermath every time. Never once did he think it could be him. He wasn't supposed to love again. Not after losing Cara. Not after the way that had changed and broken him. But here he was, lost for a woman he'd only had in his life several days and unsure how his world could turn without her. He was glad his friends knew, because he couldn't begin to put the torrent of pain into words. "Any new leads?"

"Nothing substantial yet," Wyatt said. "Reihl is canvassing businesses near the parking garage and restaurant right now. Her team is accessing local surveillance feeds and attempting to identify the imposter police officers. She's hoping that with enough footage she can track the cruisers as they moved out of town."

Jack rubbed a palm against his beard and neck. "How far has she been able to follow them?"

"As far as the highway."

Jack considered the information. "Highway cameras can track the plates from there."

"Maybe," Wyatt said. "She was only able to get partials, but it could be enough."

Jack collapsed onto the couch, willing his thoughts to sharpen. He was no use to Katlin if he was lost to emotion.

There had to be something he'd missed.

"We're going to figure this out," Wyatt insisted.

The other men grunted their agreement.

"Until she remembers what they want to know,

we've still got time," Sawyer added. "Any ideas yet on where that thumb drive might be hidden?"

Jack released a long breath, centering himself. "None."

"Well, it was smart of her to hide it."

Jack's jaw locked at the unspoken completion of Sawyer's thought. It was smart of Katlin to hide the drive *because if she hadn't, she'd be dead by now*. He raised his eyes to Griffin's memorial flag, displayed on the mantel, and willed his friend to intervene and guide him.

Someone whistled long and slow into the receiver. "Hey…" Cade's voice rose through the line. "Any chance one of you guys have a Green Beret thumb drive like the one these guys want? Or can we buy one somewhere? Maybe we can use the compromised laptop to contact the abductors, then trade the fake drive for Katlin and Maggie? We can coordinate with Reihl to set up a sting and grab the women."

Sawyer and Wyatt chimed in with feedback, opinions and logistics on the idea while Jack stared at the flag on the mantel. Griffin and Katlin had been closer than any two siblings he'd ever known. They were the best of friends. And she'd brought the flag with her even though she couldn't remember him. Why? Instinct? A sibling connection that even amnesia couldn't break? Or something else? Something *more*?

Jack stood and moved slowly to the fireplace. "She said she couldn't explain it," he murmured, as much to himself as to the men talking over one another on the call.

"What?" Wyatt asked, silencing the other voices with his question. "Jack? Who couldn't explain what?"

"Katlin," he said, taking the triangular display case off the mantel. "She brought Griffin's memorial flag from her apartment. She said she just knew she couldn't leave it behind." He turned the glass-and-wood contraption over in his hands, examining it from every angle before opening it.

"What are you saying?" Wyatt asked. "You think she remembered more than she let on?"

"No." Jack ran his fingertips reverently over the flag's material. He closed his eyes for a moment of remembrance, and in apology to Griffin in case he was wrong. Then, he slid his fingers into the neat folds of the flag until they bumped against something small, flat and hard.

Katlin had left the drive with her brother to protect, and it had worked.

KATLIN COUGHED AND gagged as an avalanche of dirt and rotten wood fragments rolled down from the small basement window and into her face. She stretched taller, up on tiptoes and undeterred. Her sore and swollen fingertips dug into the space around the ancient and deteriorating frame, where a few final shards of orange and amber light prevailed. Soon the sun would set, and they'd be cast into utter darkness, alone with the rats, according to Maggie.

Katlin hated rats.

"Here." Maggie tapped Katlin's arm with a nearly drained bottle of water. "Take a break. You're trembling."

Katlin fell back on her heels against the earth, muscles shaking from exertion instead of the cold. "Thanks." She sipped the water to clear her throat and relieve the cough.

They had to get out of there before anyone came to check on them. She'd heard voices outside the basement door earlier, but thankfully, the door had stayed securely shut while Katlin regained her faculties. It hadn't taken long for her to decide the window was the only chance of escape. Maggie agreed. She'd been digging at the decrepit frame when Katlin woke.

"I still don't understand why we're being held here," Maggie said. "I thought you were snooping on some frat kids and their side hustle. Now there's a crime syndicate?"

"Supported by our local police chief," Katlin said, returning the water bottle to her friend, and rising back onto her toes. "They'll torture me for what I know." And if that didn't work, they'd torture Maggie. They'd kill them both once they had what they wanted.

Katlin focused her fear and desperation on the work at hand, then tugged at the frame's edge until it broke. She gasped as the break sent her back several steps, arms pinwheeling and ankles turning.

"Whoa!" Maggie grabbed her shoulders to stop her fall. "What happened?"

"The frame broke." Katlin lifted a shard of jagged wood and grinned. "Now we're getting somewhere." She moved back into position, raising her new tool overhead. The sharp nose of the wood dug into the crumbling mortar.

"So you have proof about the police chief?" Maggie asked, resting a supporting hand against Katlin's back as she worked, steadying her in case she went stumbling again.

"Yeah," Katlin answered between tiny avalanches of dirt against her face. "Police chief Peterson and Donald Rosch came to a gentleman's agreement a few years ago. Rosch paid Peterson monthly, and Peterson looked the other way while Rosch and his people committed an abundance of petty thefts, some light racketeering, embezzlement, coercion and gambling. It went along smoothly for a while, then Rosch got greedy, power-drunk and belligerent with his crimes. Peterson was scrambling to cover for him, so he demanded more money for his efforts. That's when Rosch brought Dylan in on the gambling as collateral. He treated him like a king and told him not to let his dad know. Meanwhile, Rosch sent photos of Dylan to Peterson's home, implying that he'd better stay compliant or something bad would happen to his son.

"Eventually, Peterson confessed his sins to Dylan, hoping the truth would protect him, but Dylan was in too deep by then, and he owed Rosch money for gambling. So Rosch and Dylan struck a new agreement. Rosch would forgive the debt if Dylan kept his dad quiet. Dylan agreed, then Rosch stopped paying Peterson. He said the new deal was that he wouldn't hurt Dylan as long as his dad stayed onboard."

"Wow," Maggie whispered. "That's awful."

"Yeah. The bigger problem was that Peterson had become accustomed to the extra cash from Rosch, and it made things tight on his end. The reduced income caused questions from his wife, which made things even more complicated. So he came to see the attorney I was working for to talk it over off-the-record. All their discussions were protected under attorney-client privilege, but I was listening." Katlin shot a look over her shoulder. "I should have gone to the police then. I should have found someone to report this to, but I wanted the story."

Maggie rubbed her back. "At least you documented it all."

Katlin went back to work on the loose earth and mortar around the window. With a little luck, she'd be able to force the entire thing out onto the shabby grass and dirt perimeter of the home. Then she and Maggie could escape undetected. She worked furiously against the fading shafts of light on the horizon that would soon give way to moonlight.

"I recorded the conversations between Attorney Fitch and Chief Peterson from outside the closed office door, and I took everything I had to our editor. He wouldn't print it. Said it was unsubstantiated since I hadn't interviewed any of the key players. That recordings were easily and frequently manipulated. He said trying to break the case before it was foolproof could cause more harm than good, and the efforts could possibly be cast as another crooked reporter trying to make a name for herself. Ruining my career before it ever got started. Plus, I risked legal trouble for copying the files I had."

The chunk of wood Katlin had been using to dig with suddenly got lodged into the dirt and was now wedged there. Blood streamed from her hand where the opposite end broke through the tender flesh of her palm. "Argh!" She wrapped filthy fingers around the open wound, pressing hard against the flow of blood and biting her lip against the pain. "It's stuck," she said, rocking back onto the ground and working the sleeve of her shirt over the cut.

"You're bleeding!" Maggie squeaked, grabbing Katlin's hand and turning it in the fading light.

"I'm okay, but we're going to have to break the window if we want out of here before they come for us." At the pace she was currently working, she'd die of old age before removing the window any other way.

Maggie's grip loosened. "Okay. With what? There's nothing here but us and a lot of dirt. Believe me, I've searched. I couldn't even find a loose brick."

Katlin winced as the pain in her hand increased and her palm throbbed. Memories rampaged through her newly recovered mind.

She'd gone back to the law office to copy more files one night and seen Fitch inviting Rosch inside. Instead of sneaking in to eavesdrop, she'd seen an opportunity to check out an address where she'd suspected the gambling materials were stored between events. She'd reasoned that if Rosch was at the law office in Danville, he couldn't also be at a house on the west side of Campbellsville. So she'd come to the worst neighborhood in town and broken into the basement of the home where she was now being held captive. But that night the space hadn't been empty. The basement had been bursting with card tables, slot machines and roulette wheels.

She rested her head against the dirty brick wall, willing the memories to stop and her mind to focus on their escape. "I knew they used this place for storage," she whispered to Maggie. "So I came for pictures. For proof. I got everything I needed and was almost to the highway before I saw the headlights coming for me. I'll have to use my hand to break the window."

"What?" Maggie stepped back, eyes wide. "You can't. They'll hear, and how can you escape if you're all cut up and bleeding?"

Emotion pinched and stung Katlin's eyes. She squared her shoulder and shored up her nerve. "It's the only option we have left."

She'd have to take off her shirt, wrap it over her hand and hope she was strong enough to break the glass with a punch. She'd also have to hope the guards outside the basement door wouldn't hear the break.

And that would be the easy part. She couldn't afford
to injure herself any further in the process because
they had no car or phone. Once they were out, they'd
be on foot, at night, in the roughest part of town.
Alone and hunted.

Chapter Twenty-One

Jack stood shoulder-to-shoulder with his teammates and Detective Reihl. They were all gathered in a semicircle around District Attorney Martin Weaver's desk. The Green Beret thumb drive was now plugged securely into the laptop before them. It was after hours—the building was nearly empty and they were asking a lot, but given the circumstances, and the fact no one knew who could be trusted anymore, this was where they'd landed. Weaver was mentioned as one of the good guys in a file on Katlin's thumb drive, and Reihl had called in a favor to get him back to the office after he'd barely gotten home.

"What do you think?" the detective asked, pressing her palms to the man's desk. "Is this enough to build a case and make it stick?"

Weaver raised his eyes to the group, pulling his attention from the computer screen with visible difficulty. "It's enough to put Peterson away, along with several officers and Donald Rosch for a long time. And this was all collected by one junior reporter?"

Reihl tented her eyebrows, dark waves of her

hair falling over the shoulders of her black raincoat. "Yes, and she'll pay a steep price if we don't move quickly. We need warrants on Peterson, his lackeys and Rosch. If we can haul them all in, or at least get them on the run, it might remove Miss Andrews from harm's way long enough to locate and recover her."

He scraped a hand through thick salt-and-pepper hair. His gray suit was rumpled and his tie hung loose around his collar. He shook his head slowly, his expression pensive. "Heads are going to roll. The public is going to go crazy. A dirty chief of police with ties to local organized crime. It's going to be a PR nightmare."

"Let me worry about that," Reihl said, blue eyes flashing. "I just need to know you have everything you need. And that the charges will stick."

Weaver's weary eyes returned to the computer screen, scanning the files from Katlin's thumb drive. "There's a lot of information here. I'll need time to sort it all."

"But you can do it," Jack said, as much a demand as a question. They'd already been there for the better part of an hour, fielding questions and wasting time while Weaver evaluated the drive's contents. "Every minute we're standing here is a minute Katlin and Maggie could be being tortured. Or worse." His jaw tightened on the final word and heat rushed to his chest, neck and face.

Weaver released a heavy breath. "I can build the cases, but I can't guarantee protection for the women or guess how Peterson and Rosch will react to news of their pending arrests. Given the involvement of several members of the force, it'll be a miracle if they don't know we're coming before the ink's dry on these warrants." He moved his gaze to Jack. "They could decide it best to dispose of the women before the arrests."

Jack felt the world sway.

Wyatt set a steadying palm on Jack's shoulder. "We'll find her before word gets out."

"Will we?" Jack snapped, his hope slipping away. "We still have no idea where they're being held."

Weaver moved his mouse around the small pad and clicked a few times before the printer behind him rocked to life. "I might have a guess on the women's whereabouts." He turned to retrieve the paper from the printer, then placed it on the desk between them. "Rosch owns a number of properties, but there are three along the river near the exit where your friend had her accident. If I was you, I'd start with those. Each of these black dots represents one of the properties."

Jack leaned in, staring closely at the freshly printed map. An image he'd reviewed and dismissed on his ride over from the safe house. He'd assumed the marked locations were venues for previous gambling nights and hadn't given them another moment's consideration.

Now, those little black dots looked a lot like hope.

Jack turned to Reihl, renewed urgency tightening his limbs and fresh adrenaline brewing in his system. "We should split up. My team can cover two buildings at a time by breaking into pairs. I don't suppose you've got a partner somewhere we haven't met?"

"Or a team of lawmen you trust," Sawyer added, already moving toward the door.

Wyatt clapped Jack on the back and followed on Sawyer's heels.

A sly grin stretched over the detective's face as she liberated her cell phone from one pocket. "I might know someone."

Jack dipped his chin in thanks and acceptance, following his teammates toward the door. "We'll meet you there."

Reihl fell into step at his side. "Wait just a minute. You can't make an arrest and these criminals are armed. You should wait for police backup."

Cade paused in the doorway and scoffed. "Pardon me, Detective, but we're also armed. Trained. And on a mission. If we run into trouble, we'll hold our positions until you arrive or for as long as we can. We won't fire unless fired upon, but, Detective, we will get those women back."

Jack's chest swelled with hope and pride as he stared at Cade. "Oorah," he bellowed, in homage to the former jarhead.

"Oorah," Cade echoed.

Jack smiled, then swung his attention back to the small brunette detective at his side. "We'll start at the westernmost property and move east. You and your team can start east and move west when you arrive. Together, we can have all three locations cleared in minutes."

Reihl nodded, already dialing and pressing a phone to her ear.

District Attorney Weaver followed them out, a grimace on his aging face. "Some days I wonder if my work matters. Nights like tonight, I remember why I ran for this position to begin with. Good luck to you all. I'll be waiting for your good news."

Jack turned to him and extended a hand. "Thank you." He offered a strong shake before breaking into a sprint to the parking lot.

If Katlin was in one of the properties on that map, he would find her.

Tonight.

KATLIN STRIPPED OFF her long-sleeve T-shirt, the frigid chill of the basement raising goose bumps over her exposed skin. Blood oozed from her wounded palm, the puncture deeper and more severe than she'd initially thought.

"Maybe there's another way," Maggie said, her small frame unsteady beneath Katlin.

"Just hold me tight. I'll count down." Katlin steadied her breath and secured the material around her closed fist. She'd climbed up to sit on Maggie's shoulders for added height and a better angle to break the glass, and hopefully not her hand, with the punch. "Ready?"

A low rumble of voices rose in the home above them, growing louder before stopping on the other side of the basement door. Katlin held her breath, temporarily frozen and staring across the dark expanse to the place where a fresh shaft of light bled under the door.

"Hurry!" Maggie whispered, her body swaying. Her fingers gripped Katlin's calves tightly enough to leave ten tiny bruises. "Now!"

Unable to think past her friend's urgent pleas and the men about to catch her in an attempted escape, Katlin pulled back her fist, twisted slightly at the waist, then snapped her hand forward, the way Griffin had shown her. The way he'd promised would flatten anyone bold enough to lay an unwanted hand on her. She could only hope the old glass pane was weaker than the average jaw.

The glass shattered upon impact, falling in blades over her tightly wrapped fist, raining down the wall and into Maggie's hair. And some landed on the blessed ground outside, reflecting the newly risen moon.

Before she'd breathed her first full breath of night air, Maggie had released her calves in favor of boosting her through the newly opened escape hatch. Katlin landed partially in and partially out of the window, her head and shoulders under the stars. She winced as glass dug into her bare stomach, arm and torso. Pain screamed through her.

"Go!" Maggie cried. "They're coming! Go!"

The door rattled, and a tall slice of light cut into the darkness behind her.

"Hey!" a man's voice boomed. "What was that? What broke in here?"

Katlin dug her fingers into the scrubby grass,

broken glass and earth, pulling the rest of herself through the window while Maggie pushed and shoved her legs.

"Go!" she called, loudly now. "Run!"

Katlin spun on her stomach in the dirt and debris, thrusting blood-streaked arms back through the empty windowpane. "Not without you."

She and Maggie locked fervent gazes as blinding light flooded the room. Two men stood at the top of a rickety-looking flight of steps. A bulb on a chain swung before them like the pendulum of a ticking clock.

Maggie jumped for Katlin's hands and held on tight. Using their connection like a rope, she walked her feet up the old block wall until she was close enough to be dragged outside.

Katlin leaned away, feet planted in the hard earth, and heaved. Maggie's head and shoulders burst through the window, her legs kicking behind.

Slurs and curses burst through the basement as the men tore across the room, already down the flight of stairs.

A large hand hit the dirt beside Maggie's knees as she struggled to find her bearings. A second hand clutched her shoe and jerked her back by a foot.

Maggie's scream filled the night, and Katlin lurched after her, heart pounding and mind scrambling.

"I've got you now," he growled.

"No, you don't!" Katlin screamed back. She clutched her friend with her good hand, and searched the ground around her with the other. Her aching fingers curled over a palm-size stone and she brought it down on his hand with a stomach-tossing crunch.

The attacker fell back with a wail, releasing Maggie in an instant.

"Outside!" he yelled. "Get them!"

Footfalls hit the interior wooden steps at a run.

Katlin pulled Maggie to her feet. "Are you okay?"

Maggie nodded and gasped for air. "Yeah. Thank you."

"Good." She unwound the shirt from her hand and stretched the bloody fabric back over her sliced-up torso, then grasped her friend by the hand. She cradled her opposite, gashed wrist and forearm against her chest, fighting against the throbbing pain and burn. She sent up a silent prayer as the flowing blood seeped through her shirt and warmed her skin beneath. "Let's go."

Together, they stumbled down the dark and narrow alleyway outside the old home, ducking behind a dumpster when a set of headlights cut across the property's front lawn.

Maggie's teeth chattered in the darkness as the home's front door slammed open, and two men burst onto the aging and tilting porch, guns drawn. "More of them?"

"I don't know," Katlin said. "I don't want to find out."

A large black SUV appeared a moment later, roaring over the sidewalk and climbing half onto the craggy, unkempt grass. The vehicle's front doors opened and figures dressed in black took up position behind the barriers. Their guns were drawn, as well.

"Whoa." Maggie's grip on Katlin tightened. "We've got to move."

Katlin agreed, but following through was harder. Her body was weak, her head light and vision blurry. Her stomach rolled with each unsteady step as she bumbled along at Maggie's side, attempting to put distance between them and the pack of armed men.

"You're bleeding," Maggie moaned, tugging at her cradled arm. "Oh, my goodness, you're covered. Is that all from the cuts on your stomach and chest?"

"No." She opened her mouth to say she'd gashed her arm, was losing too much blood and needed to sit down, but gunshots rang out behind them, effectively silencing that story.

Maggie screamed.

Katlin's knees buckled, and her shins collided with the hard and broken asphalt.

"No, no, no," Maggie said, hefting Katlin upright and swinging her burning, bleeding arm around her shoulders. "We can't stop now. You need a hospital."

Katlin bobbed her head in agreement, her vision nearly gone. She trusted Maggie to guide her. She pressed on, forcing every awkward stride for the sake of the friend she'd unintentionally dragged into her mess.

"You can do it." Maggie whispered the words like a low and repetitive chant, whether to Katlin alone or for the benefit of them both, she couldn't say. She dragged as much as guided Katlin along the alley and into a dark and narrow space between buildings while the men on the lawn exchanged shots behind them. "Maybe we can find someone willing to let us use their phone," Maggie said. "Maybe someone will give us a ride, or we'll see a police cruiser on patrol."

"No…" Katlin choked on the word, struggling to work her failing tongue. "No police. We don't know—"

Her words were cut short once more. This time, as the broad beam of a flashlight landed on them and another man dressed in black stepped into their path.

He lowered the beam and reached for Katlin as her eyes rolled back and her legs gave out.

She'd never been so sorry. For the path she'd chosen. The decisions she'd made.

For putting Maggie in harm's way.

And for never telling Jack Hale that she loved him.

Chapter Twenty-Two

Jack's heart seized as Katlin's eyes rolled and her legs gave out. He lurched forward in the darkness, cursing the broken streetlamps and whoever had done this to her.

Maggie stumbled under Katlin's collapsing weight, a fierce and determined expression on her small, livid face. "Let her go!"

"I've got her," he said, working to keep his voice low and strong, even as Katlin's body fell against his, lifeless and limp. "I've got you, too," he vowed, locking gazes with Maggie in the moonlight. "You're going to be okay." He tugged the black balaclava below his chin, exposing his face from eyebrows to neck. "We're here to bring you home."

Maggie's lips trembled, and a small sob broke free. Her eyes were wild with terror. Her face and hair filthy. Her ruddy cheeks streaked with tears. "Jack?"

He offered a stiff, affirmative dip of his chin. "My team's here. Help is on the way. We've got to go." He swept an arm under Katlin's legs and raised her off the ground, cradling her body against his as a broad mass of clouds raced across the sky, blotting out the moon and stars. *Better cover for them*, he thought. *And better cover for their enemies, as well.*

"Stick to the shadows," he instructed. "I don't know how many of Rosch's men will respond to the gunfire." He turned back the way he'd come, scanning Katlin's face as he moved, straining for better sight in the darkness. Her breaths were short and shallow against his chest. Her skin cold to his touch. And a dark stain coated her shirt, hands and arm. He supposed it was too much to ask that she'd simply collapsed from dehydration, fatigue or fear.

"Are you hurt?" he asked Maggie, who rushed along at his side.

"No," she cried. "I'm fine. Katlin's hurt. She's cut and bleeding. She needs a hospital."

Jack's chest constricted painfully as he gave the woman in his arms another, closer look, willing the dark patches over her clothes and skin to be dirt, like the marks on Maggie. "What happened? How was she cut? When?" He changed trajectory, crouching slightly as he jogged closer to the nearest working streetlamp and into its light. He motioned for Maggie to follow. They needed to be careful not to expose themselves to any of Rosch's men.

Another nearby round of gunfire made Jack hunch his shoulders and hurry his steps. A heartbeat later, his stomach pitched at the revelation made beneath the streetlamp.

Maggie's sobs intensified at the illumination

of Katlin's body, coated from her torso to wrist in blood. Her forearm was sliced to the elbow. The wound was jagged and deep. Similar cuts were visible on her stomach and side, where her shirt had ridden up as he'd carried her. "Get my phone," he barked, straining his neck for a look into Maggie's eyes. "Hip pocket. Dial 911. And try to keep up."

The moment Maggie retrieved the phone, Jack broke into a run.

Maggie followed, reporting the situation to a dispatcher as they ran. "She punched out the window to save us," she explained, detailing the horrific experience after noting their whereabouts and general situation. "One man grabbed my foot and she hit him with a rock. I think she broke his hand," she rambled. "She saved our lives, and now I think she might die!"

The final word nearly brought Jack to his knees. Katlin's skin was as pale as the moonlight, and losing her would surely stop his own heart. He couldn't let it happen.

Wouldn't let it happen.

Sirens raged in the distance, ripping their way through the night. Carousels of emergency lights wound high in the sky, drawing closer with each of his rampant heartbeats.

Cade was out of his seat the moment the waiting SUV came into view. "What the hell happened?" he yelled, breaking into a sprint for Jack and Maggie.

Jack opened his mouth to speak, but the words didn't come. Instead, he felt the heat and sting of emotion in his eyes, nose and throat. He couldn't lose her.

Would he lose her?

A riot of voices boomed through the night, rising on the air outside the home where Wyatt and Sawyer had been forced to open fire on a pair of men racing out with guns drawn.

Jack and Cade had taken the opportunity to find an alternate route of entry. The armed men at Rosch's property might as well have been beacons to Katlin and Maggie's location. Jack had taken to the alleyway, prepared for a stealthy extraction. Cade had remained at the wheel for a fast escape once the women had been recovered.

Katlin wasn't supposed to be hurt.

It wasn't supposed to turn out like this.

"On the ground!" Detective Reihl demanded in the distance, her voice strong and familiar.

Backup had officially arrived.

"Hands behind your back!" she demanded as the sound of doors being kicked open echoed through the night.

Cade darted into the road, playing chicken with the first ambulance on the street. He swung both arms overhead, shouting for the driver's attention. "Here!" He shoved the fingers of one hand into his mouth and whistled.

The ambulance redirected, bypassing the officers and arriving cruisers. Past Detective Reihl, who was cuffing men on the home's front lawn.

The EMTs piloted a gurney in Jack's direction.

"What do we have?" the female asked, eyeballing Katlin as Jack placed her on the padded stretcher.

"Female, twenty-six," Jack began, fighting the tidal wave of fear and pain attempting to drag him under. "Multiple lacerations. Critical blood loss..." His ears rang as he ran down all that he knew about Katlin's condition, and let Maggie fill in the gaps he couldn't.

He watched, frozen and helpless, as they pressed an IV needle into her ghost-white skin, cut off her shirt, checked her vitals and cleaned her seemingly endless number of wounds.

He watched as they loaded Katlin into the bus, then pulled up Maggie with them.

And he watched as the ambulance drove away. Taking his heart with them.

KATLIN WOKE TO the blinding fluorescent light of a hospital. Her ears rang, and her eyes blurred as nearby voices spoke her name.

"Jack?" She'd parted her lips to speak. To ask how she'd gotten there. To ask if Maggie was okay. To request someone contact the police if they hadn't already. But the only thing her mouth and mind could manage together was that one precious word.

Jack.

The thought sent a spike of fear through her chest. Her gaze jumped from the myriad of blinking, beeping machines near her head to the door along the opposite wall. She'd been held captive. She'd gotten free. Gotten out with Maggie, and then there had been gunshots. "Jack."

"She's awake," someone whispered, drawing her attention from the closed door to a cluster of people at the end of her bed. Maggie beamed and covered her mouth, but didn't move. Instead, she slid her eyes in the direction of the most beautiful thing Katlin had ever seen.

Jack turned, eyes bright with relief and gratitude as he moved slowly in her direction. "Hey," he said, his voice as warm and light as the sun. "How are you feeling?"

Katlin felt her toes curl beneath the scratchy hospital blanket. "Better now." She bit her lip and did her best not to blush at the way he was looking at her. As if she was the most beautiful thing he'd ever seen, too. "Do I know you?" she teased.

Jack's lips twitched and curled at one corner. "Funny."

The relief on his handsome face sent shivers down her spine, and when he came close enough, she reached for him.

He pressed his mouth to hers with such care and reverence that she turned to mush beneath his touch. Then he peeled her hands from his scruffy, bearded cheeks and planted a feather-light kiss on the bandaged palm.

Her fingertips curled over the warmth left behind by his touch and tears swam in her blurring eyes. "I love you," she whispered, biting her lip and watching the flecks of green and gold grow more brilliant in his hazel eyes.

His mouth was on hers again in an instant. A long press at first, followed by a multitude of lighter ones. "I love you, too. I should have told you sooner."

Maggie squealed from her position at the end of Katlin's bed, and the Fortress men muttered things like "get a room."

"Katlin!" a familiar voice called, making her heart tighten in her chest.

Jack turned, giving view to faces she'd longed to see more than she'd realized.

"Mom? Dad!" she cried, unable to stifle the sudden punch of emotion. "How are you here?"

Her mother and father rushed to the bed, sending Jack out of the way.

"Baby," her mother wailed. "I'm so sorry we weren't here." She pressed warm palms to Katlin's cheeks, tears pooling in her brown eyes. "We've been on one plane after another since we got Jack's call." She pressed a kiss to Katlin's forehead, then rested her head against her daughter's. "We were so scared. What if we had lost you?"

"I'm okay," Katlin said, hearing the unspoken fear in her mother's words.

What if her parents had lost her, too? The way they'd lost Griffin.

"Jack saved me," she said, daring a look at her hero, who was shaking hands with her father while his teammates claimed their part in Katlin's saving.

Jack winked in her direction, and Katlin eagerly

replayed his perfect words. *I love you, too. I should have told you sooner.*

Maggie bounced through the ring of brawny men, and threw her arms around Katlin's mom. "Hi, Mrs. Andrews," she said, stepping back with a wide grin. "Katlin cut herself saving me. She nearly died, but she's fine now. She's been out cold for hours, but before that she single-handedly broke up a gambling ring and took down a local crime boss and crooked police chief."

Her mom's mouth fell open. Her father frowned. Together, they turned to stare at Katlin.

"I had help," she said, waving an arm to the crew of newfound family before her, and a best friend she'd loved since college.

Her father moved in close and squeezed her unbandaged hand, then traded a look with her mother.

She turned her attention to the group gathered around Katlin's bed. "You were all there?"

Everyone nodded.

Her parents widened their eyes in wonder. "Well," her father said. "Let's hear it. We want to know everything. Including how we can ever repay you."

The room broke into a flurry of voices, each with their own tale of how the last week had gone down. Jack's teammates spoke of shoot-outs and corruption. The loss of Katlin's memory and the death of her poor boss, Attorney Fitch, killed by one of Rosch's henchmen. Maggie told of her capture and their daring escape. Jack ended the mash-up of stories with praise for Detective Reihl, her team and the district attorney, who'd made the arrests possible. "Thanks to them, it's safe for Katlin to live her life however she chooses again." He stroked her arm with the backs of his fingers and looked into her eyes. He lowered his voice, turning his attention to her alone, and whispered, "I hope it will be with me."

She luxuriated in the sound of that. Living her life freely with Jack. Could there be anything better?

"What?" her dad asked, his voice sharp, bordering on harsh.

"Jack?" her mom asked, flipping her gaze from her husband, to her daughter, then to Jack.

"That nearly sounded like a proposal," her father said, crossing his arms and narrowing his eyes. "We talked about this."

Katlin's mouth sank open. "You talked about this?"

Jack nodded. "When I spoke with him by phone."

"I was on a plane en route from Libya," her father added. "I wasn't sure if I should give him a blessing or a beating, until I heard him out."

"Dad," Katlin gasped. The heat of embarrassment and anticipation scorched paths across her cheeks. "Stop."

"So, which was it?" Maggie asked. "Because he doesn't appear to have been beaten," she said out of the side of her mouth, wiggling her eyebrows at Katlin.

Katlin covered her face, a hodgepodge of emotions battling for the forefront in her mind. "I'm so sorry," she told Jack. "We don't have to talk about this right now," she whispered, casting a bashful glance over the quiet, painfully attentive guests.

But she hoped he'd still want to talk about it later.

Then Jack lowered to one knee and took her hand in his.

"Shut. Up," Maggie stage-whispered, linking her arm with Katlin's mother's and bouncing onto her toes.

A collective rumble rolled over the Fortress men as Jack fixed Katlin with a pointed stare. "I hadn't planned on doing this right now, but I also promised myself I'd never again put off telling you how I felt or how much you mean, so here it is." His voice cracked, and he cleared it before pressing on. "Katlin Andrews, you are the most fierce, resourceful and beautiful woman I have ever known. You healed and filled my broken heart when I was perfectly content with being miserable, and in doing so, you brought me back to life. I don't want to spend a minute of my future without you in it."

Katlin's throat ached and her eyes welled with unshed tears. "Jack," she croaked. "What are you doing?"

"Shhh!" Maggie exclaimed, and the group chuckled.

Katlin covered her mouth with shaking fingers, and filled her lungs with air.

"You trusted me to protect and fight for you the first night we met," Jack said. "If you'll take one more chance on me now, I promise that I will live a life dedicated to making you glad you did, every single day. For the rest of my life."

She sniffled, and a nurse passed her a box of tissues. A crowd of hospital staff filled the open doorway.

Jack rose to his feet and moved in close. "Katlin," he implored, leaning nearer still. "Marry me."

She nodded, unsure she could speak.

He stroked her cheek and kissed her nose, then raised her hand to his lips. "I'm afraid I'm going to need a verbal answer, for the record."

"Yes." Her laugh was interrupted by a fresh press of his lips.

And the room erupted in cheers.

The flash of a camera went off somewhere behind her closed eyelids, and she didn't care if the photo ended up in the paper or on the evening news. She loved Jack, and he loved her, and she melted deeply into the man who would be hers alone for the rest of their very long lives together.

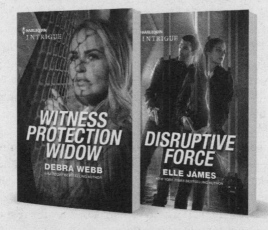

Makena needed medical attention. That part was obvious. The
tricky part was going to be getting her looked at. He was still
trying to wrap his mind around the fact Makena Eden was
sitting in his SUV.

Talk about a blast from the past and a missed opportunity.
But he couldn't think about that right now when she was injured.
At least she was eating. That had to be a good sign.

When she'd tried to stand, she'd gone down pretty fast and
hard. She'd winced in pain and he'd scooped her up and brought
her to his vehicle. He knew better than to move an injured
person. In this case, however, there was no choice.

The victim was alert and cognizant of what was going on.
A quick visual scan of her body revealed nothing obviously
broken. No bones were sticking out. She complained about her
hip and he figured there could be something there. At the very
least, she needed an X-ray.

Since getting to the county hospital looked impossible at least in the short run and his apartment was close by, he decided taking her to his place might be for the best until the roads cleared. He could get her out of his uncomfortable vehicle and onto a soft couch.

Normally, he wouldn't take a stranger to his home, but this was Makena. And even though he hadn't seen her in forever, she'd been special to him at one time.

He still needed to check on the RV for Mrs. Dillon…and then it dawned on him. Was Makena the "tenant" the widow had been talking about earlier?

"Are you staying in town?" he asked, hoping to get her to volunteer the information. It was possible that she'd fallen on hard times and needed a place to hang her head for a couple of nights.

"I've been staying in a friend's RV," she said. So, she was the "tenant" Mrs. Dillon had mentioned.

It was good seeing Makena again. At five feet five inches, she had a body made for sinning underneath a thick head of black hair. He remembered how shiny and wavy her hair used to be. Even soaked with water, it didn't look much different now.

She had the most honest set of pale blue eyes—eyes the color of the sky on an early summer morning. She had the kind of eyes that he could stare into all day. It had been like that before, too.

But that was a long time ago. And despite the lightning bolt that had struck him square in the chest when she turned to face him, this relationship was purely professional.

Don't miss
Texas Law *by Barb Han,*
available December 2020 wherever
Harlequin Intrigue books and ebooks are sold.

Harlequin.com

HIEXP1120

HARLEQUIN

*Heartfelt or suspenseful,
inspiring or passionate, Harlequin
has your happily-ever-after.*

With new books published
every month, you are sure to find the
satisfying escape you know you deserve.

SIGN UP FOR THE
HARLEQUIN NEWSLETTER
Be the first to hear about great new
reads and exciting offers!

Harlequin.com/newsletters